TRACK THE MAN DOWN

TRACK THE MAN DOWN

RAY HOGAN

THORNDIKE
CHIVERS

This Large Print edition is published by Thorndike Press, Waterville, Maine, USA and by BBC Audiobooks Ltd, Bath, England.
Thorndike Press, a part of Gale, Cengage Learning.
Copyright © 1961 Ray Hogan.
Copyright © renewed 1989 by Ray Hogan.
The moral right of the author has been asserted.

LIBRARY OF CONGRESS CATALOGING-IN-PUBLICATION DATA

Hogan, Ray, 1908–
   Track the man down / by Ray Hogan.
      p. cm. — (Thorndike Press large print Western)
   ISBN-13: 978-1-4104-2112-8 (hardcover : alk. paper)
   ISBN-10: 1-4104-2112-0 (hardcover : alk. paper)
   1. Large type books. I. Title.
PS3558.O3473T68 2009
813'.54—dc22   2009033902

BRITISH LIBRARY CATALOGUING-IN-PUBLICATION DATA AVAILABLE

Published in 2009 in the U.S. by arrangement with Golden West Literary Agency.
Published in 2010 in the U.K. by arrangement with Golden West Literary Agency.

U.K. Hardcover: 978 1 408 47710 6 (Chivers Large Print)
U.K. Softcover: 978 1 408 47711 3 (Camden Large Print)

Printed in the United States of America
1 2 3 4 5 6 7 13 12 11 10 09

TRACK THE MAN DOWN

1

The road south, out of Santa Fe, had been long and tiresome. Ben Dunn, slouched in the corner seat of the stagecoach, let his body roll and toss with the swaying, pitching vehicle and stared across the vast carpet that was New Mexico Territory. In one more hour they would reach Crawford's Crossing. There he would quit the groaning Concord, pick up his horse, and begin the final twenty mile trip home.

The coach veered suddenly, reeled to one side as it plunged into an arroyo. Dust puffs exploded from the corners behind the seats, and the vehicle cracked and popped loudly. Outside, on the box, the driver shrilled his curses, fought with the leather ribbons laced between his fingers.

"Git on there, Brownie! Hi-eeee-ah! Blaze! Git along, you jug-headed broomtails!"

The coach righted itself, snapped back into line as the four-up lunged into the harness, took up the slack. Dunn, displaced from his corner by the lurching motion, readjusted himself. He was glad the long journey to the Capitol, in Santa Fe, was about over with.

It seemed like he had been riding for weeks instead of days. And he would never have made the trip, had there been any choice. But the matter of the dispute that lay between himself and Isaac Pope, whose quarter-million acres of Diamond X Ranch lay west of his, had to be settled.

Pope was dying, and if the problem waited there would never be any straightening it out with Jack Marr, who would inherit the spread once the crusty, old rancher was gone. It would be settled now. The small canyon that ran between them, the bone of contention, was clearly on his Box B property. The spring from which flowed a steady stream of clear, sweet water was his. He had with him a certified map from the land office to prove it. Once Isaac Pope saw the map, it would be ended; for, despite his rapacious nature, Pope was a fair man. He would claim nothing that was not rightfully his.

Dunn was glad the quarrel was soon to end. The peace and contentment he had found on the Comanche Flats, those past three years, had afforded him a way of life far different from the precarious and wary existence he had endured before coming there. He did not want it to end.

When he purchased and moved onto the small, ragtag ranch he renamed the Box B, he had been quite alone on the Flats. There were only two other inhabitants within reasonable distance: Abner and Hopeful Loveless, an elderly couple who lived in a shack at the foot of Comanche Mountain. They actually were within Dunn's property, but he permitted them to live on the small plot of ground they had chosen and eke out a livelihood from the soil.

After a time he hired Loveless during periods when he needed help, usually the spring and summer months. Dunn's herd was small, never over a couple of hundred steers, a half a dozen horses. He intentionally kept it that way. He had little use for money since his needs were few. Once a year he sold off twenty or thirty head of beef and that provided him with enough hard money to purchase necessities and pay Abner Loveless for what services he had rendered.

He had seen little of Pope and his right hand man, Jack Marr, who, Abner once told him, was no real kin. Pope had no family of his own and had taken in Marr to raise as a son. Together they had built up the Diamond X to become the largest and most respected ranch in that part of the territory.

They had left Ben Dunn alone, and all had gone well until the change took place. With it had come the dispute over the spring. Pope decided to move his ranch buildings off the Flats, to a new, more desirable position at the foot of Comanche Mountain. Trouble had come swiftly: sharp words with Marr; several clashes with Diamond X riders. An attempt to reason with old Isaac got him nowhere. It all resulted in the hurried trip to Santa Fe for a copy of the land office map.

"Hi-eee-ah, Brownie! Spot! Blaze! Satan! Git along! Git along!"

Dunn glanced out the window. He was the only passenger, and now he moved across to the opposite seat in order that he might see better. The country was taking on a more familiar look. They were drawing nearer to Crawford's Crossing. He recognized the low run of red-faced bluffs to the south, and the lengthy, flat-lying ridge that paralleled the road which led to his ranch. He straightened up and stretched his wide shoulders. It wouldn't be too long now.

It was near mid-morning when they pulled to a halt before the squat, adobe buildings where Tom Crawford operated a combination stage stop, general store and livery stable. It was no regular breaking point in the line's schedule, so there was no horse change. It was merely a pause in the long run to El Paso.

Dunn swung down from the coach, waited while the driver dug out his valise from the iron-railed baggage area behind the box. He caught the bag when it dropped, turned away. From the gallery that fronted the store, Crawford greeted him.

"Mornin', Ben. Glad you're back."

Dunn stepped up onto the porch, followed the man into the store. He said, "Any particular reason?"

"Could be," the storekeeper answered. "Sabine and Pete Frisco were by here early today. Way they were talkin', somethin' must have happened over at your place."

Dunn stiffened as alarm moved quickly through him. Bibo Sabine and Pete Frisco worked for Pope — or, rather, for Jack Marr. Both men were hardcases, accustomed more to using a gun than a rope.

"Any idea what it was? They say anything about Abner?"

Crawford scratched at his stubbled chin. He shook his head. "Nope. But I gathered they gave him a rough time over that spring

11

you and Pope are bickerin' about. You get that proof you went after?"

"Dunn patted his inside pocket. "Right here," he said. He moved to the front of the store, threw his glance across the way to Finley's Saloon. If the two Diamond X men were still around, they would be found there. There were no horses at the rail. The stage driver, having tarried long enough to quench his thirst, was just coming through the doorway.

"They didn't hang around long," Crawford said, reading his mind. "Headed back for Pope's after they got themselves a few snorts."

Dunn said, "I see. My horse ready?"

"Waitin' in the stable," Crawford answered. "When I heard the stage comin', I told Manuel to saddle him up. Figured you'd be in a hurry."

"Obliged," Dunn said and reached for the door handle.

"That wire and other stuff you ordered got in," the storekeeper said then. "You want to take it now, you're welcome to use my wagon."

Dunn said, "No time. Better get to the ranch and see if Abner's all right. I'll drive in tomorrow and pick it up."

"Good enough. It'll be ready to load."

His bay horse was waiting for him when he circled Crawford's building and entered the low-roofed stable, a hundred feet or so to its rear. He gave his thanks to the Mexican hostler and swung onto the saddle. Anger and worry hammered through him in a steady throb, and he lost no time covering the score of miles that lay between his Box B Ranch and the stage stop.

A feeling of relief coursed through him as he rode down the last slope. His small house, with its scatter of outbuildings still stood in the clearing. They had not been damaged or burned, as he had feared. Now, if Abner were all right . . .

The old rider came from the barn at that moment. He limped noticeably and the left side of his veined face was swollen. He halted in front of the wide doors, lifted his hand in greeting.

"Afternoon, Son. See you made it."

Relief flowed through Dunn. Loveless was not badly injured but the anger within the rancher did not lessen. He dismounted, looked at the older man closely. "This come of Sabine's work?"

Loveless said, "What? Oh, you mean this here jaw of mine. Yeh, Bibo sort of pushed me around some. Not bad. I been slapped around before, and lots worse than this."

"Bibo's a big man," Dunn commented, sarcasm heavy in his voice. "What was it all about, the spring?"

"The same," Abner replied. "Saw your waterin' pond gettin' low. Rode up to see what the trouble was. Pope's bunch had dammed up our ditch and dug a new one that ran to their side of the hill. Was changin' it back when Bibo and Pete Frisco come along."

The simmering anger within Ben Dunn exploded in an oath. "I'm going to straighten this out with Pope, once and for all!" he said. "You get home all right?"

"Sure," Loveless said. "You ridin' over to see him right now?"

"Right now," Dunn echoed. "Got the proof I need to convince him that the spring is on my land. I'll let him look it over, then tomorrow we'll fence off the canyon. Be no more of this. I was willing to share the water with Pope, but now he and his Diamond X bunch can go hang!"

"Spring ain't big enough to share, anyway," Loveless observed.

"Big enough if they didn't try to hog it," Dunn said. He moved back to his horse, stepped to the saddle. "You go on home. When I get ready to start stringing that fence, I'll come for you."

Loveless said, "Good enough. Now, watch

14

yourself at Pope's. Like walkin' around in a nest of rattlesnakes."

Dunn favored the old man with a wry grin. "If we're goin' to keep on living around here, I guess this is the time to start pulling some fangs."

"That's for dang sure!" Abner Loveless said. "Good luck to you!"

It was near the supper hour when he rode into the wide, hard-packed yard of Pope's Diamond X Ranch and halted before the main house. He dismounted, looped the reins of the bay about the hitch rail. He wheeled slowly, let his eyes sweep over the buildings of the ranch. All were good, well built structures, and in excellent repair. Pope had a fine place. He stepped up onto the gallery, made his way to the door and knocked.

It opened almost immediately. Evidently Jack Marr had been standing just inside for some time. He was a tall man, probably twenty-five years old, which made him about the same age as Dunn. He had dark eyes and hair, a narrow face accented somewhat by hollow cheeks. His mouth was small, his teeth too fine and white. Those things, linked with a thin, aquiline nose, destroyed any claim to handsomeness and bestowed, instead, a definite cunning to his countenance. He regarded Ben with surly suspicion.

"What's on your mind, Dunn?"

"Little matter I mean to take up with Pope," Ben answered, and stepped by Marr. He entered a large room, cluttered with heavy, leather-covered furniture, a huge oak table with lion's-paw legs. There were mounted game heads on the walls and tanned skins upon the floor.

"I look after things here," Marr said coldly. "Take it up with me."

Dunn shook his head. "No, I came to see Pope. Either lead me to him or I'll find him myself."

Marr studied Dunn's set jaw for a brief time. Then, he said, "All right. Follow me."

He started toward the back of the house, the polish on his blood-colored, handmade boots glowing dully in the subdued light. Marr wore the best, when it came to clothing. His broadcloth suits cost more than most cowboys made in three months of hard work, Ben guessed.

"In here," Marr said in his flat voice.

They had reached an open door at the end of the hall. Inside the room Ben saw Isaac Pope lying on a bed. His first glance at the rancher showed him that the man, indeed, was in a bad way. His skin was like old paper, yellowed and cracked. He was little more than a skeleton with lusterless eyes sunk deep into his skull. He had changed greatly since their last meeting at the disputed spring. At that time Pope had been well enough to sit in a saddle and snarl his orders. Now, it appeared doubtful that he could even raise his head.

"Who's there? What do you want?"

Pope's question was a dry, impatient crackle of words. Ben moved beside the bed. He drew the land office map he had obtained in Santa Fe from his pocket.

"It's Dunn," he said, answering the old rancher. "I've come about that spring you claimed was on your land. I brought a map to show you that it's not. It belongs to me."

Isaac Pope fastened his baleful glare upon Ben. "Map? What kind of map?"

"One the land office made up. Shows your exact property lines. That spring's on my side, just like I told you."

The rancher struggled to a sitting position. He extended his gnarled hand for the paper. "Show me," he ordered. "You show me where the line is."

Dunn held the map before him, indicated the area in question with a forefinger. He traced the boundaries of the two ranches. Pope studied them for several minutes. Apparently satisfied on that score, he examined the official markings on the stiff paper, assured himself of the map's authenticity.

"Reckon you're right, Dunn," he said, and sank back onto his pillow. "Look at it, Jack, so's you'll know."

Marr stepped in closer. He scarcely glanced at the map. "I see it," he said.

"That settles it," Pope stated, releasing his grasp of the paper. "It's on your property, Dunn. I'll make no more claim to it. And you forget about it, Jack. Tell the rest of the crew to do the same."

Marr said, "Sure, Pa. Not much good to us, anyway."

"Water's always a good thing in this country!" Pope crackled. "But that ain't none of ours, so forget it."

"Sure, Pa," Marr said.

Dunn refolded the map, thrust it into his pocket. He started to say something to Pope about the state of his health, to express a hope that he would soon be better. But he changed his mind. Isaac Pope was not the sort of man you conveyed such sentiments to.

Instead, he said, "I'll be going, Mr. Pope. Glad we got this ironed out with no big trouble."

The rancher threshed about beneath the

thin coverlet. "All right! All right! I said it was your's. Now get out of here and let me rest!"

Dunn wheeled and returned to the hall. Marr followed. When they reached the front room, Marr reached out, laid his hand on Ben's arm.

"I expect to keep on using water from that spring, Dunn. Don't go doing anything foolish, like fencing it off."

Dunn knocked Marr's hand aside. "There will be wire across that canyon, soon as I can string it," he stated. "Don't want to see you or any Diamond X rider, or any of your stock on my side again. That clear?"

Marr's thin face was expressionless. "Don't put up any fences, Dunn. This is the only warning I'm going to give you!"

2

Ben Dunn was in Crawford's Crossing early that next morning. Well before daybreak, he had harnessed up his team of bays to the light spring wagon, and made the trip to the supply point. Crawford had expected him. He had the supplies out on the gallery, waiting to be loaded.

"Anything serious happen yesterday?" the merchant asked as he helped Dunn stow the boxes of groceries and spools of wire in the vehicle. "Abner get hurt bad?"

Dunn said, "Sabine roughed him up a mite. Little matter I've got to take up with Bibo, first time I run across him."

"Could be right soon," Crawford said. "He and Pete Frisco rode in a couple hours ago. They're over in Finley's Saloon now, easin' their thirst. You get squared around with old Isaac?"

Dunn nodded. "We had an understanding," he said, non-committally. He shoved the last box of supplies into a corner of the wagonbed, drew a light tarp over it all to keep out the dust.

From down the road came the sound of running horses: the clatter of metal and cracking of wood. Crawford drew a thick, silver watch from his vest pocket, squinted at its face.

"Stage's right on time," he said.

Dunn grunted, straightened up. He threw his glance across the way to the saloon. "All of a sudden I got me a thirst," he said. "Think I'll pay Finley a visit."

Crawford eyed the rancher speculatively. "You right sure it's a drink you're lookin' for?"

Dunn grinned. "Man never knows who he's going to run into in a saloon," he said and stepped off the porch.

The stage whirled into the yard in a boiling cloud of dust. It skidded to a halt. The driver wrapped the reins around the whipstock, swung down. Dunn paused, watching him turn to the door and open it.

"Crawford's Crossing, lady. This is the place."

A flamboyantly-dressed girl of seventeen, or possibly eighteen, appeared. She was not particularly pretty but she had clear, blue eyes, dark hair and thick, equally dark brows. Her mouth was wide, with generous lips; the soft creaminess of her skin was proof she was no permanent inhabitant of that frontier land.

The driver assisted the girl to alight. He looked at her closely. "Ma'am, you sure this the place where you want off? Ain't nothin' here but that store and that saloon, over there."

Her face was pale. "I thought it would be a town."

"No town closer than a hundred miles. You want to go on?"

Ben Dunn watched the girl, waited for her answer. He was having a difficult time getting her classified in his mind. The dress she wore was a bit garish and bold. It was cut far too low at the neckline, much too short at the hem. Yet her face belied the thought. There was none of the customary commonness to her; there was no harshness to her features, no hardness in her eyes. It was as though she were dressed in another's garments — an angel in the cloak of a fancy woman.

"No, I'll have to stay," the girl said, firmly. She took her small carpetbag from him, tucked it under an arm.

Bibo Sabine and Frisco, unaware of Dunn's presence on the far side of the coach, strolled into the yard from the saloon.

"What you bringin' us, Harry?" Sabine called to the driver.

"Lady bought a ticket to here," the man replied. "All I know about it." He centered his attention on the girl once more. "You sure you don't want to go on, ma'am?"

She drew her light, cloth stole more closely about her shoulders. "No, this is where I want off."

"Go on, Harry," Sabine said. "Lady's made up her mind to stay, and I'm sure goin' to make her welcome."

The stage driver climbed back onto his perch. He unwound the leather ribbons, glanced to Crawford. "You got anything for me, Tom?"

"Nothin'," Crawford answered.

The driver shouted at his horses and the stage lurched and plunged out of the yard. The girl watched it leave and then turned to Crawford, a look of helplessness on her face.

Bibo Sabine said, "Right this way, girlie. The saloon's over here." He swaggered to her side, took her by the arm.

Dunn saw horror and fear spring into her eyes. He stepped away from his team, moved swiftly up to Sabine. He took the cowboy by the shoulder, whirled him around. He drove a rock-hard fist into Sabine's jaw. The Diamond X rider yelled, went backwards and sprawled in the dust.

"Get up!" Dunn said. "Got a couple of things to settle with you."

Sabine scrambled to his feet. He glared at Dunn, his thick shoulders hunched forward, arms akimbo. A low mutter of curses trickled from his thick lips.

"Looked for you yesterday at Pope's," Dunn said. "Seems you want to slap old men around. Like Abner Loveless. How about trying it on me?"

Sabine said nothing, simply lunged. Dunn stepped lightly to one side. As Sabine went by, he smashed him to the ground with a down-sledging right. The cowboy came up fast, whirled. Dunn doubled him over with a sharp left to the belly, straightened him up with a right to the chin. Sabine gasped, staggered back.

"This one's for Abner," Dunn said and sent a straight right to the cowboy's nose.

Sabine went down hard. From the edge of his eye, Ben Dunn saw Frisco move in on the right. He wheeled to face the man. His heavy six-gun came magically into his hand. Pete Frisco halted.

"You name it," Dunn said, softly.

Frisco waited out a long minute. He shook his head. "Reckon it ain't for me."

Dunn said, "All right. Load up Sabine and get out of here."

Frisco crossed over, helped the dazed Sabine to his horse. Dunn waited until they had ridden from the yard and then turned to the girl. The anger within him had dwindled, but there was still a faint edge to his voice.

"Somebody supposed to meet you here?"

She said, "No. Nobody knew I was coming. Can you tell me where the Pope ranch is?"

Dunn stared at her. From the porch Crawford said, "About thirty-five miles due west. You goin' to walk?"

The girl did not smile at the weak jest. "I didn't think it was so far. Isn't there a stagecoach —"

"Not going in that direction," Dunn said. "You sure it's the Pope place you want?"

"Yes, Isaac Pope."

Dunn said, "Well, my place is about fifteen miles this side. If you're willing to ride in my wagon, I'll take you there."

Relief showed in her face. "Thank you," she murmured. "I'll be ever so grateful, Mister — ?"

"Ben Dunn," he supplied and handed her

up to the wagon seat.

"Mr. Dunn," she finished. "My name is Laura. Laura Pope. I'm Isaac Pope's daughter."

Dunn froze where he stood, stared at the girl in astonishment. Crawford, leaning against the door frame of his building, snorted.

"Buzzards are already beginnin' to gather."

Dunn flung a sharp glance at the storekeeper. "Never mind, Tom," he said. He circled the wagon, climbed up onto the seat beside the girl. He gathered up the reins, slapped the horses on their broad backs. They leaped forward and the vehicle rolled out of the yard, settled into the ruts that struck into the west.

After a few minutes, she said, "You don't believe me, do you? About being Isaac Pope's daughter, I mean."

Dunn was busy with the horses. After a brief time he answered her. "Who am I to question it? You say you are; as far as I'm concerned, you are. Guess you caught me by surprise with it."

"But I am Laura Pope! Is it so strange that he should have a daughter?"

The bays felt good and were fighting him, anxious to run. Dunn gave in, let them have their way. The road across the flat plain was fairly good. Later, when they drew nearer to the mountain, he would have to slow them down, make them take it easy.

He said, "Always heard Pope had no family. Reason he took in Jack Marr."

"Jack Marr? Who is he?"

"The son of some friend of Pope's. Brought him into his house when he was a kid. Raised him like he was his own son."

The girl considered that. "I see. What did that man back at the store mean — about the buzzards gathering?"

His eyes on the road, Dunn explained. "Pope's dying. Probably won't be long now. His place is worth a lot of money. Crawford meant there probably would be a lot of people showing up, wanting to get their fingers in the pie."

"I didn't know he was sick," Laura said, wearily. "But that's the way it would be. It's only what I should expect."

He glanced at her, noted the hopelessness in her eyes. "Meaning what?"

"After sixteen years I finally learn who my real father is, only to find him dying, maybe already dead."

A covey of blue-feathered quail suddenly whirred off from beneath the horse's hoofs. The team shied violently, carried the wagon out of the road in a wild detour. Dunn went forward in the seat. Crouched like a Roman chariot driver, he got them back into the shallow ruts. The sun was climbing higher in its clean, cloudless arch, and it had turned increasingly warmer. When the bays were again in line, sweat stood out on Dunn's brow in large beads. He brushed it away with a sweep of his hand.

"Lot of people going to think like Crawford," he said. "Be natural, with you showing up right at this time — and wearing clothes like you have on."

She looked down at her dress. "The only ones I had, and they were my mother's."

"Your mother's?" he repeated, frowning.

"Yes. She died about six months ago."

"Sorry to hear it," he mumbled.

The team was running free down a long, gentle grade. He wrapped the reins around the ship, removed his leather jacket, and tossed it into the rear of the wagon. He looked ahead, searched his memory and the land for a suitable place to halt for lunch. There was a shallow arroyo, he recalled, a few miles on. It offered a scatter of thin cottonwood trees, but no water. Still, it would be better than open ground.

"Expect you're hungry," he said. "We'll pull up and eat soon."

She made no reply, simply stared out over the plain. He glanced at her, wondered if she had heard.

"This country is so big . . . so lonely," she said, almost to herself. "It's filled with emptiness."

Dunn laughed. "Reckon that's about as near right as you could say it. But you get used to it. Once you have, you'll never like any other place."

"Have you lived here long?"

"Around here since the war."

"The war," she repeated in a falling voice, "it changed so much for all of us."

They reached the cottonwoods shortly after that and halted. Dunn picketed the team on a small stand of short grass, turned to prepare lunch. From his saddlebags under the wagon's seat, he obtained a blackened coffee pot and a sack of dark beans. He crushed a handful between two rocks, dumped the grains into the container. He added water from the canteen, and set it over a quick fire. While it came to a boil, he got the crackers, some tinned meat, and a can of peaches from the groceries Crawford had furnished him.

"Not much of a feed," he said to the girl when it was ready. "Reckon it will do until we reach my place."

She ate in silence and when they were finished, she went quietly about cleaning up and restoring the provisions and equipment to their customary containers. That done, she turned, looked at Ben Dunn with grave eyes.

"Is this dress really so bad?" she asked, as if she had been thinking about what he had said. "I thought it was pretty."

"It is," he agreed, "but hardly what a man would expect his daughter to be seen in."

"I had nothing else to wear," she said, sitting down beside him. "I want you to know that. The way I may look now has nothing to do with what I am."

"I could see that," Dunn said. "But other men will think different."

She said, "I know. There were a few times on the trip out here —"

"People have a way of judging others by their appearance. Generally wrong."

"True, but I would like you to know the story. I want you to understand."

"It's all right," he said. "If it hurts to talk about it, let it ride."

"But I want you to hear it! You should have the straight of it. You're the only friend I've had since I left home. You're entitled to the truth."

He said no more. He fished a match from

his shirt pocket, struck it. He held the small flame to the tip of his cigarette, inhaled deeply. The sound of the horses cropping at grass was a steady crunch on the still air. High overhead a Mexican eagle soared in lazy circles.

"I never knew my father, my real father, I mean. I was born here, on his ranch but when I was about two years old my mother took me and ran off with a drummer. She couldn't stand the terrible loneliness of this country. She was a St. Louis girl and not used to the sort of life Isaac Pope offered her."

Laura paused, glanced at Dunn. He was watching the gliding eagle, cigarette drooping from one corner of his long lips.

"I don't recall much until I was six or seven. I do remember that we traveled around a lot, went from town to town. I thought Corey Phillips was my father. Everybody always called my mother Mrs. Phillips. I know now they were never married because she and Mr. Pope were never divorced.

"We were all happy and then the war came along. Corey was killed in one of the very first battles. Things just sort of went to pieces for us after that, and we finally ended up in a mining town in Pennsylvania where mother took a job in a saloon.

"I guess I knew it wasn't a very nice job and she knew it, too. But we had to live and eat and there weren't any jobs for women, especially after the war was over. My mother never let me see where she worked, but I knew about it. I stayed at home, kept house and went to school. I used to make fifty cents a week looking after the babies that belonged to two of the women who worked with my mother. It wasn't much but it helped a little. Mother never was able to bring home much money."

"She must have been a fine woman," Dunn said. "Takes a lot of courage to keep on going, like she did."

Laura gave him a grateful smile. "About a year ago she took sick. She got to where she couldn't go to work and we had to depend on the charity of friends. She grew worse, and we both realized she was going to die."

The girl halted abruptly, looked away. Dunn said, "You don't have to go on," in a kindly voice.

She sat up straighter. "I want to!" she said. She waited out several moments, continued. "That was when I found out about my real father, Isaac Pope. Mother told me the whole story, said I was to go to him after she passed on. She said he would never forgive her but that he would hold nothing against me, his own daughter. She wrote a letter to him so he would know who I am. I have it here in my bag, along with a picture she gave me. Would you like to see them?"

Dunn shook his head. "They're for Pope, not me."

"After she was gone, I got ready to leave. There were only a few dollars, little else but I sold what I could to raise the fare. Mother's friends all helped, donated what they could. I heard that someone passed a hat at the place where mother worked to take care of Molly's daughter, as they called me. I finally got enough together to buy a ticket. There wasn't any left over for clothing, so I wore a dress of my mother's, along with some things her friends gave me. That's why I'm dressed as I am. I had no other choice.

"It has been a long ride from Pennsylvania and I'm glad it's about over with. I'll see my father, tell him what mother told me, and show him the letter and picture. If he welcomes me, I will be thankful; if not, I'll just have to go on, find myself a job of some sort, somewhere.

"Maybe out here in this new country, a girl can find a decent job. I don't want anything from my father except a home — and that only if he wants to give it willingly.

If he doesn't — well, I'll manage some way."

Dunn glanced at her. "The kind of work you'll find in this country won't be much different from the kind your mother found in Pennsylvania."

"Then if that's the answer, that's the way it will be. I can be as strong and as brave as my mother, if I have to. I don't want it that way, but I've already learned we don't get to have things the way we'd like."

Dunn reached over, laid his hand upon hers. "Maybe it will all work out for you," he said, gently. "Don't worry too much about it. Isaac Pope is a hard man, but he's honest and he's fair. He'll do the right thing. I'm not very welcome around his place, but if there's anything I can do to help —"

"Thank you," she murmured. "Just being my friend and listening to me is all I ask."

They packed up and moved out shortly after that. The afternoon wore on. They reached the bottomlands, as the area was generally called, rolled swiftly along a rocky, brushlined road. Dunn's Box B spread was less than a mile distant now. It was almost full dark and night would be upon them by the time they arrived at his place. He was debating the best course to follow: whether to stop at his ranch; eat and rest for a time;

or simply obtain fresh horses and continue on to Pope's. Laura was tired, he knew, but likely she was anxious to complete the journey.

He turned to her. "You feel up to riding fifteen miles more tonight? It will have to be on horseback —"

A gunshot suddenly blasted through the dark hush. Off to their right and close at hand. Dunn grabbed for his gun, tried to hold in the bays. From a remote corner of his memory, a single name rushed forward, exploded from his lips.

"Greavey!"

A wild yell followed the shot. The bays swerved sharply, nearly overturning the wagon. Dunn forgot his weapon, sawed at the reins as he tried to bring the frantic team back onto the road.

"Hold on!" he yelled as the wagon bounced and rocked over the uneven ground.

More shooting erupted. Dunn heard the shrill whine of bullets. The bays, thoroughly frightened now, plunged down the narrow alleyway between trees and shrubbery. The wagon swayed dangerously, whipped back and forth like a string in a stiff breeze.

"Look out!"

Dunn shouted a warning. A large rock was

suddenly in the road before them. He tried to swing the wagon to one side to avoid it. The left side, front wheel smashed into it, crumpled with a loud popping sound. The hub hit into the soft earth and hung momentarily. The vehicle left the ground and flipped over with a crash.

3

Ben Dunn struck on all four. Groceries and other supplies showered down around him like rain. One of the spools of wire came up against his leg, almost knocked him flat. He ignored it all, glanced wildly about for Laura. He saw her; a crumpled shape off to his right.

He got to his feet, raced to where she lay. The team, hampered now by the wagon's dead weight, had stopped a dozen yards down the road. He dropped to the girl's side, slipped his arm under her shoulders and raised her carefully.

"Laura!" he said. "Laura!"

She opened her eyes slowly, stared up at him. "What happened —"

"Everything's all right now," he replied. "You got a rap on the head when the wagon went over. How do you feel?"

"A little dizzy," she said. "Are you hurt?"

He shook his head. "Was lucky." He raised

his eyes, looked about. "Whoever it was, he's gone now. We're only a short way from my place. Rest here until I unhitch the team, then we'll go on. I'll, pick up the pieces tomorrow," he added ruefully, surveying the scatter of items.

He left her, went to the heaving bays and freed them. They were quiet now. He led them back to Laura. She was sitting up when he reached her. She was badly shaken, he could see.

"Can you ride?" he asked, kneeling beside her.

She said, "I think so. I'll try."

He helped her onto one of the horses. She took a firm grasp of the harness. "Who was it that caused the runaway? Do you know?"

"Didn't see anybody. But I've got a pretty good idea. Hold on. We don't have to go far."

He walked ahead of the horses, led them down the road through the darkness. He was thinking of how strange it was that Jay Greavey, an enemy of the past, should have come into his mind when the ambush exploded about them. Likely it had been Bibo Sabine and Pete Frisco, endeavoring to get even for the incident at Crawford's Crossing.

They reached the Box B, entered the yard.

He halted the bays in front of his small, three room house and turned to Laura. He reached out, took her under the arms and swung her to the ground.

"Wait here. I'll go inside and light a lamp."

He went immediately to the door, pushed it back, and entered. The lamp was on the table and he struck a match to its wick. The room filled with a warm, cheery glow. He wheeled to call Laura, found her standing in the doorway watching him.

"You can use that room there," he said and pointed to his own sleeping quarters. "Soon as I look after the horses, I'll fix a bite to eat."

The girl did not move. "I didn't expect to stay the night."

He saw the uncertainty in her eyes. "I don't think you're in any condition to make the ride. It's a hard fifteen miles."

He crossed the room, threw open the door that led into the bedroom. "You'll be safe. You can lock the door, if you like. I'll lay myself a pallet on the kitchen floor."

"I won't be afraid," she said and stepped by him.

He went into the yard, took the bays into the barn. He removed their harness and they walked into their customary stalls. He threw down some feed for them and came back into the open. Suddenly deciding he should do something about the groceries he had left strewn around the wrecked wagon, he took his wheelbarrow and returned to where the mishap had occurred. He loaded up all things that might draw wild animals during the night, added to them Laura's valise and his saddlebags, and went back to the house.

When he entered, he was pleasantly surprised to see that she had taken over. She had built a fire in the stove. On it coffee was already beginning to boil, and the frying pan was popping with hot grease. She half turned when he came in, smiled at him.

"Felt I should do something," she said. "Hope you don't mind. Will meat and potatoes be all right? And corn meal muffins?"

"Sounds good to me," Dunn replied. "You feel up to it?"

"Certainly," she said, and resumed her work. "Are you finished outside?"

"All done. And I brought your bag."

He finished stowing away the supplies on the shelf. The room was beginning to fill with tantalizing odors of frying meat and potatoes, the rich flavor of coffee. He pulled back a chair, seated himself at the table. Without asking, she poured him a cupful of the steaming, black liquid.

"Food won't be long," she said.

He found himself enjoying the moments, the easy relaxation. He watched her, busy at work; he listened as she lightly hummed the words of an old war tune. He found himself thinking; *this is the way a man should live,* and wished it might be so for him.

"Don't you get lonely here, living all by yourself?" she asked suddenly.

He thought for a moment. "Maybe so. Never gave it much notice until now. When you're busy and got a lot of work to do, it just never occurs to you. Right now, however, I'm seeing how much I've missed."

She smiled at him. "I take that as a nice compliment, Mr. Dunn," she said. "Thank you. I guess we're ready to eat."

Both hungry, they ate in silence. To Ben Dunn the meal was delicious, surpassing by far any he had eaten in the restaurants along the trails, or that he had prepared for himself. He had fried meat and potatoes innumerable times but never had they possessed the savory qualities of these. It was the woman's touch, he decided.

He told her so, and added, "Leave the dishes. I'll take care of them tomorrow. You ought to rest. That was a bad knock you got on the head."

"I'm all right," she said. "Besides, we'll need them for breakfast. Drink your coffee. I made plenty. It will take me just a few minutes to clean up."

Dunn produced his old pipe, tamped it full with rough-cut tobacco. He lit it, settled back. A man never realized what he was missing — until he had a sample of what genuine living was.

The faint scrape of leather outside in the yard cut through his thoughts. It brought him to his feet instantly. In one swift motion he killed the light in the lamp, whirled to the door.

"Greavey!"

The name again unconsciously blurted from his lips. He dropped to a crouch, opened the latch. He jerked the door wide, plunged into the night, gun ready in his hand. There was no one there. The yard was empty. And then he heard, faintly, the hollow, retreating hoofbeats of a running horse. Whoever it had been was gone.

He wheeled slowly, returned to the house. Sweat had gathered on his forehead and tension still showed in the hardness of his gray eyes. And there was a measure of wonder in them, also; wonder as to why Jay Greavey was on his mind. Was the gunman somewhere near? Was intuition, somehow, voicing a warning within him?

Laura waited silently for him to turn up the lamp, resume his chair. She refilled his cup. The dishes were unfinished. She ignored them.

"Too late to see who it was," he murmured.

She sat down opposite him. "Who is Greavey? Twice I heard you mention his name, like he was someone you perhaps feared."

Dunn stirred. His brow clouded. "I don't think I'm afraid of him. It's just the waiting, I suppose, expecting him to come someday and have it out."

Horror spread through her eyes. "He wants to kill you? Why?"

He did not immediately answer. He studied his pipe moodily, then, "I gunned down his brother, Tom. I went after him to take him on a murder charge. He decided to fight."

"And now he's looking for you. Were you a lawman of some sort?"

"In a way. Out here they call them bounty hunters. Not exactly a kindly name. I went after the outlaws the regular lawmen left alone. For the reward."

"Did you always have to kill them?"

He shook his head. "They had a choice.

There were some who came along with no trouble, but not many. Because they are desperate men, they usually choose to fight rather than surrender and face a hangman's rope. You hear talk about bounty hunters being bloodthirsty killers. It's not exactly the truth. An outlaw picks his own way to go.

"I didn't want to kill Tom Greavey. He forced my hand. And when it was all over and I looked down at him and saw he was just a kid, something happened inside me. He could have been my own younger brother. It made me a little sick and I quit bounty hunting right then. I'd saved up a little money and started looking for a place where I could settle down and work the land, raise some cattle. Guess I figured that by doing so, I could get it out of my system."

Dunn paused. His pipe was out and he lit it again. "It worked pretty well — except you don't ever forget the things that have happened. The past is always there, no matter how hard you try to put it out of your mind. Someday Jay Greavey will come along and we'll settle our score. And when he does, it will be finished, one way or another."

She shuddered at his words. They had shocked her. He realized that as he sat there.

"Don't let it bother you," he said. "It's the way of things out here. A man picks his road to travel and stays with it, come hell or high wind. He's got nobody to blame but himself for the reckoning he someday has to make."

"But it's all so cold, so inhuman! To just sit and talk about killing, or being killed. Back east —"

"Back east is a different world," he said, "and people there have no real idea of what it takes to stay alive in this country. Now, you had better get some rest. We've got a hard trip ahead of us in the morning, and it won't be on the seat of a wagon."

4

Despite an early start, it was near ten o'clock that next morning when Laura and Dunn rode into Pope's Diamond X Ranch headquarters. Ben had offered her a pair of his old, faded denims, in the interest of comfort, but since they were several sizes too large, she had declined.

Several of Pope's hired hands strolled out into the yard as they drew up to the hitching rail that fronted the main house, but none came forward to meet them. Dunn dismounted, helped Laura to do likewise.

She glanced around uncertainly. He could see she was uncertain, almost fearful of what lay ahead. He smiled at her. "Everything will be all right."

Her chin became firm. She thanked him with her eyes for his encouragement. "I ought to freshen up a bit before I see him. Where could I go to wash up and get the dust off?"

Dunn pointed to a door further along the side of the building. "That's the kitchen. Pope has a Mexican woman cook. Why don't you see her?"

Laura said, "Thank you," and turned away. Abruptly she halted. "And thank you for bringing me here, and everything else. I hope I haven't caused you too much trouble."

"Forget it," he said. "Was my pleasure. Good luck."

She continued on toward the rear of the house. Beyond her, in the yard, Dunn saw Bibo Sabine and several Diamond X punchers give her their undivided attention. Sabine, a thin-faced, dark-eyed gunman of sorts who generally hung close to Marr, said something. They all laughed.

Dunn felt anger rise within him. He strode swiftly across the open ground, hauled up before the cowboy. Sabine's grin died when he saw Dunn coming. He glanced about at the men beside him, his face now sullen and stiff.

Dunn said, "Appears I didn't make things clear enough at Crawford's yesterday."

He stepped forward, drove his fist into Sabine's jaw. The gunman staggered back, came up against the man directly behind him. Both went down in a tangle of legs and arms.

"Damn you!" Sabine yelled. "I'm gettin' tired of you —"

Dunn's pistol came into his hand with a swift, fluid motion. The cowboys back of Sabine froze. The gunman scrambled to his feet. Anger distorted his face, turned it a beet red.

"Who you think you are?" he demanded.

"I'm the man who's going to put a bullet into you next time you come sneaking around my place," Dunn said flatly. "And if I was sure you were the one that spooked my horses last night, I'd take it out of your hide!"

"Who says it was me?" Sabine demanded.

"Nobody, but I got a good hunch it was you. This time I'll let it pass. I see you on my property again, however, it'll be a different story."

"Reckon I'll come and go as I please," Sabine said in a defiant tone.

"Not across Box B land," Dunn snapped. "That goes for all of you."

"What goes for all of us?"

At the sound of Jack Marr's voice, Dunn turned slowly to one side. He met the tall man's gaze coldly. "The 'no trespassing' sign on my land. You can't see them, but they're there. And they mean every man who works for Diamond X."

Marr shrugged. "You've said that before. Who's disputing it?"

"Ask your gun ranny there," Dunn said. "Let him tell you."

He swung his hard, pressing glance over Sabine and the others, as if assessing their intentions. Apparently satisfied with what he saw, he slid his pistol back into its holster. With no further words, he pivoted on his heel and walked back to his horse. He mounted up, and with the horse Laura had ridden on a short lead rope, he headed out for his ranch.

He rode at a leisurely pace, came into his yard around the middle of the afternoon. Abner Loveless awaited him. The white-haired old puncher waddled out from the barn on bow legs to greet him. He still limped some and the side of his face was now thoroughly discolored.

"Get your business tended to?"

"All done," Ben replied.

"You convince Pope that spring was yours?"

Dunn headed into the barn with the two horses. "No sweat at all. Showed him that land office map and that's all there was to it. He gave Marr orders to stay clear."

"Good. Glad to hear it's settled. Brung you over a mess of the missus' stew. Set it there on your stove."

"Obliged. Sure appreciate it and you tell your wife so. All this woman cooking is going to spoil me for my own, if I don't look out."

Loveless helped him remove the gear from the horses. That done he said, "How so?"

"Had a woman — a girl here last night that fixed me a fine supper. And breakfast, too."

"A girl?" the old puncher echoed, his brows going up. "Wondered about that extry horse. Who was she and what was she doin' here?"

"Brought her in from Crawford's, where she was stranded. She was going to Pope's."

"What for?"

"Says she's his daughter, Laura."

Loveless was speechless for several moments. He recovered, scratched at his head. "Didn't recollect old Isaac ever had a family. Course there was the time when I didn't know him. You right sure she's kin?"

Dunn nodded. "Said she was. That's all I know about it."

Finished in the barn, they moved toward the doorway. Dunn said, "Appreciate your looking after things while I was away. I'll

50

settle with you at the end of the month."

"Forget it," Abner replied. "Were no work to it." He followed Dunn into the yard, shaking his head. "Old Isaac's daughter, eh! Sure does beat all. Reckon Jack ain't goin' to like it much."

"For sure," Ben agreed. "You busy tomorrow? Thought I'd get that wire up around the spring, if you'll help."

"Be glad to," Loveless said. "Late in the mornin' suit you?"

"Fine. And don't forget to thank Hopeful for that stew. *Adios*."

"I'll remember," Abner said and climbed stiffly onto his horse. "So-long."

Dunn spent the rest of the day bringing in the remainder of the supplies scattered around his wrecked wagon and doing small chores about the place that needed tending to. When darkness came, he entered the house. He put a fire under the stew and the coffee pot, noting the neat and orderly fashion in which Laura had left his kitchen.

He wondered how she had made out with Pope, if she had been able to convince the old rancher that she was his daughter. He hoped so. He would like to think that, at least, Laura would have a good home. He went to bed early and fell asleep quickly.

Shortly after sunup he was in the barn

saddling up his buckskin, when a sudden rush of hoofs outside brought him up sharply. Unconsciously, his hand dropped to the gun at his hip, as he assured himself that it was ready. He walked into the open. Four riders were drawn up in the yard: Marr; Pete Frisco; Sabine; and a man he did not know. He looped the reins of his horse over the rail, continued slowly toward the Diamond X men.

They watched him approach, waited until he was standing only a few paces away. Marr spoke.

"Pretty slick deal you tried to pull, Dunn. Only it's not going to work."

Ben shrugged. "You don't want to take that land office map I brought back as proof, then you'd better ride to Santa Fe and look it up yourself," he said, believing their visit had something to do with the spring.

"Not talking about that," Marr stated. "I'm talking about that woman you tried to ring in on us as Pope's daughter."

Dunn said, "Well, isn't she?"

"You know damn well she's not! I saw through that deal quick. You knew Pope was dying and you come up with this idea to get your hands on his ranch. You and that girl are working together. You figured you could palm her off as his daughter. Then when he dies, the two of you could take over."

Ben Dunn's shape stiffened as anger swept through him. "That's a lie, and you know it! I never saw the girl until she climbed out of the stage at Crawford's. I brought her along with me and took her to Pope's because she didn't have any other way to get there."

"A good story. You going to tell me now that she didn't spend the night with you here before you brought her over?"

"Sure she stayed here. My team got spooked and ran away; the wagon was turned over. She was hurt a little. Besides, it was too late to go on."

Ben Dunn was growing more furious with each passing moment. Marr's accusations lashed him like a metal-tipped whip.

"Where you got her hid?" Marr demanded. "In that shack or there in the barn?"

"She's not around here," Ben said. "Haven't seen her since I left Pope's. And I don't expect to. Now, get off my place and stay off!"

"Not so fast, friend," Marr said coolly. "You overplayed your hand this time, Dunn. Time I'm through with you, you'll wish you'd never seen that girl before. Take a look in the barn, Pete. You try the shack, Bibo.

She's around somewhere."

Ben Dunn's pistol came up, centered on Marr. "Be the wrong thing for them to try," he warned.

From off to the left another voice drawled, "Be the wrong thing for you, too, mister. Just drop that iron."

A fifth man, one he had not noticed. He was stationed out of sight, beyond the house. Ben let his weapon fall to the ground. He looked up at Marr.

"You're a fool. The girl's not here."

"Maybe. We'll see. And if she's not, we'll take you on to the marshal, anyway. We'll find her later. She won't get far."

"Marshal?" Dunn said, surprised. "What for?"

"Murder," Jack Marr replied. "For sticking a knife into Isaac Pope last night and killing him."

5

Ben Dunn stared at the tall Marr. Words failed him completely for the moment, and in the hush that followed the accusation, the only sounds to be heard were the dry creaks and squeals of leather as Bibo Sabine and Pete Frisco swung from their saddles to do Marr's bidding. Then the fifth man with the rifle drifted deeper into the yard, halted a few steps from Dunn. He reached down, picked up Ben's pistol, thrust it into his own belt.

At last Dunn spoke. "You're a bigger fool than I thought, Marr," he said, "or else you're framing this. You know I had nothing to do with Pope's death."

"Only thing I know," the tall man said, "is that it all adds up. You and your lady friend schemed up a way to get the Diamond X by claiming she was his kin. Then you got Pope out of the way so you could take over."

The wild fury within Ben Dunn had

blown itself out. Now, there was only a hard core of seething anger. He glanced about through shuttered eys. Marr had not drawn his pistol, nor had the fourth man. The only gun on him was the rifle held by the rider who stood a few paces away. He calculated his chances for escape; the greatest risk lay in the fact that no horse, upon which he might flee, was handy. And it would be senseless to attempt a break on foot. If he could somehow move fast enough to get his hands on the rifle . . .

Bibo Sabine came from the house at that moment. He halted just outside the door. "She ain't in here, Jack."

Marr said, "Look around the yard. Maybe she's in one of the sheds or hiding in the brush."

Sabine turned to do as he was told, walking in that awkward way of saddlemen, unaccustomed to being on foot and disliking every moment of it. Pete Frisco emerged from the barn.

"Ain't nobody in here," he yelled. "Looked good."

Marr nodded. "All right. Bring Dunn's horse up here. Then help Bibo."

The thick-shouldered Frisco led Ben's buckskin to where they had gathered. He handed the reins to Dunn, wheeled about and struck out across the yard after Sabine.

"Mount up," Marr ordered. "Don't get any ideas, unless you want to die quick. I'd as soon haul you in dead as alive."

"Expect you'd like that better," Dunn said dryly and stepped into his saddle.

Again he looked about. He was considerably better off now. On a horse his chances for escape were much improved. But there was still the problem of having no gun. He was not looking beyond the immediate need to get away, to get free of Marr and his riders. After that was accomplished he could sit back and think the matter through, decide what must be done.

The minutes dragged slowly by. Sabine and Frisco were somewhere behind the barn, poking about in the brush and weeds. The fourth man stirred uncomfortably as the gradually-rising heat and inactivity began to wear at him.

"Sure don't look like she's around here."

Marr said, "Maybe not, Charlie, but we're going to be sure. Got to find her."

"You figure she come this way. You find tracks or something?"

Marr shook his head. "Didn't look for any. Where else would she go? Only other place she knew around here was Dunn's. She wouldn't just take off across the flats."

"Reckon you're right," Charlie mumbled.

Sabine and Frisco appeared at the far corner of the barn. Marr pivoted his attention to the man with the rifle. "Get your horse, Harvey."

The cowboy wheeled off at once, started for his mount which stood, apparently, somewhere in the brush beyond the house. Ben Dunn realized his moment was suddenly at hand. He threw a glance at Sabine and Frisco, another at the departing Harvey. He was the dangerous one. Ben set himself in the saddle.

It was a good twenty-five yards to the nearest stand of shrubbery — and possible escape. But he would chance it. He would act the instant Harvey was out of sight and while Frisco and Sabine were still at the far side of the yard. At that moment he would have only Jack Marr and the cowboy called Charlie to contend with.

Tension built with the fleeting seconds. It would be a tight squeeze. With each step away Harvey took, Frisco and Sabine drew a pace closer. He sought to estimate the position of the two gunmen when Harvey turned the corner of the house. Somewhere near the yard's dead center, he figured. He would be within range of their hand guns. He must endeavor to put Marr and Charlie in between them and himself when he made his move.

From the tail of his eye he saw the rider with the rifle reach the corner, turn. Methodically he counted, allowing time for Harvey to get a distance beyond. He drove spurs into the buckskin. The startled horse plunged forward, straight at Marr.

Dunn yelled, adding to the confusion. The buckskin veered to avoid colliding with Marr's gray which shied off frantically. He came up against Charlie's mount, reared suddenly.

"Get him!" Marr yelled, savagely fighting his horse.

Bibo Sabine's shout came from the yard, close by. Dunn, crouched low on the leaping buckskin, did not look around. These were the critical moments — the time it would take him to gain the shelter of the brush. He expected to hear the crash of gunshots. There were none. Evidently he had succeeded in maneuvering Marr and Charlie into a position where they blocked the two gunmen. Harvey, the rider with the rifle, was the big question; would he hear, turn and reach the corner of the house in time to lay down a shot?

The buckskin was covering ground in huge strides. It was a short distance to the brush but to Dunn it seemed like miles. Back of him he could hear Marr cursing in a steady flow, interspersing the scathing words with commands. A gun suddenly cracked through the morning. Charlie, he suspected. The bullet droned by, thunked dully into a small tree just beyond Dunn. He crowded down tighter on the buckskin's heaving body. Only ten feet more . . .

He reached the first stand of brush as several guns opened up. Wild bullets, clipping viciously through the leaves and other foliage behind him, told him they could not see his exact position. He kept low, raced on, driving the buckskin recklessly down a shallow ravine that drained away to the right.

Marr and the others were getting underway. The shooting ceased and he was aware of the pounding of their horses in pursuit. But he breathed easier. In a chase, on his own land where he was familiar with every foot of ground, his chances were better than good. But he must try to keep from their sight; no man could outrun a bullet.

He swept down the arroyo, swung hard left, where it flattened out into another. He did not look back. There was no need. The hammering of the running horses kept him well informed. He looked ahead. He was heading back toward Comanche Mountain now. There was no safety out in the open, on the flat country; the rugged, rocky and thickly overgrown canyons and ridges of the mountain itself were his safest bet.

He pressed the buckskin for more speed. The game little horse responded and drove on. But he could not be expected to maintain such a pace for long. The grade was growing steeper, the footing becoming more uncertain. The possibilities of the horse stumbling increased with every stride.

Dunn risked a look over his shoulder. He must know how near Marr and the others were. He saw them as he turned. They were just rounding a curve in the arroyo he was following. It was their first glimpse of him. Three guns broke out as one.

Ben again heard the whine of death as the bullets whirred past, this time much too close. He saw spurts of dust ahead as they struck the ground, heard their scream as they ricocheted off into space. He jerked the buckskin sharply to one side, threw a screen of brush across their rear. The horse was beginning to heave, to tremble from his running. He could not go much farther.

A narrow corridor between high-piled rocks appeared to his left. Without hesitation, he veered into it. It slanted gently back downgrade, gave the buckskin some relief from his climbing. The passageway ran a dozen yards, ended abruptly against a thick stand of scrub oak. Dead end! The horse slid to a halt.

The hair on Ben Dunn's neck began to prickle and stiffen. He would be trapped if Marr and his riders were to spot the turnoff and elect to follow it. He slipped from the heaving buckskin, crept forward a few steps and listened. Off to the right, he could hear them thundering up the trail. Marr's voice shouted something. It was almost drowned by the horses, and Dunn could not distinguish the words.

The sound swept on. He realized a moment later that they had missed the turn and were continuing on up the slope of Comanche Mountain. He trotted back to his horse, mounted up. He returned to the main trail, headed downward. They would soon discover their error, he knew, but he would not be where they could find him. He knew exactly where he would go — on the topmost ridge of the mountain.

6

He allowed the buckskin to pick its way slowly along the foot of the mountain, keeping well hidden within the maze of brush and rock. Higher up on the slope, he could hear faintly the shouts of Jack Marr and his men as they combed through the rough area. They had split, it seemed to him, and were now searching individually. He was safe, at least for the time. He was far below them, making a long swing toward the opposite end of the mountain.

He wished there had been time to get himself a gun. But the only available one was back at the ranch. And that would have meant exposing himself. The Diamond X men would certainly spot him and come boiling down the slope to box him in before he could get away a second time. He would have to do without a weapon. All he could do was to stay hidden, permit Marr and his riders to hunt themselves out. When they would be gone, he could move about freely.

He reached the spring over which he and Isaac Pope had quarreled, halted there long enough to water the buckskin and have a drink himself. When that was done, he headed up a long canyon that slashed diagonally across the body of Comanche Mountain. High, steep walls here closed in on him from two sides, but he had no fears. Marr was a considerable distance to the east of him and could, in no way, look down into the gash where he moved.

It was familiar ground to Ben Dunn. He had climbed the narrow, canyon trail before, knew it would lead him eventually to the base of the rimrock that capped the mountain. From it he could reach the only break in the ridge whereby a man could gain the summit. It was an old, game trail, likely unknown to anyone but himself and the long-eared mule deer that used it.

At its upper end, the walls of the canyon began to lower. The trail became a series of rock ledges. Dunn dismounted; From that point he proceeded on foot. It was unsafe to ride the buckskin any further. The horse would have a difficult enough time maintaining his footing on the smooth, rain-washed rock without the extra burden of a rider.

It was well into the afternoon when he reached the top, broke out onto the broad, grassy meadow that lay behind the ridge. It was a beautiful plateau, thrust high into the heavens, clear and blue as a flawless diamond. Grass was knee-deep everywhere, shifting back gently back and forth with the whim of the breeze like a vast sheet of undulating silver. It extended for miles in all directions, carpeted the crater-like top of Comanche Mountain.

Ben allowed the buckskin to wander out into the grass. He cut back, climbed a slight peak and turned his attention eastward, into the direction where Marr and his men would be. Flowing out beneath him and the many colored facets of the rimrock, was the first, steep slope of the mountain. It ended several hundred yards down, where it bulged slightly and resumed a more gentle descent. The entire face of Comanche Mountain was studded with pines, firs and other growth as well as with rocks of varying sizes. This prevented him from locating Marr and the others.

But by studying the land and its formations, and from his personal knowledge of the country, he eventually sighted the general area where he could expect them to be. He marked that particular section in his mind by sighting a dead juniper tree that clung precariously to the edge of the rim. He dropped back to the buckskin, mounted, rode eastward through the turbulent sea of grass until he was opposite the marker. There he again turned loose the horse, who would not drift far in such excellent grazing. Dunn then made his way to the ridge.

Before he was fully on the rim, he heard a man's hoarse shout. He removed his hat, dropped flat to the ground and crawled to the juniper. He looked down. At first he saw nothing. Moments later he watched two riders emerge from the trees, halt in a small clearing far below.

The man on the gray horse unquestionably was Jack Marr. The other he could not recognize at such a distance. As he watched, a third man entered the open ground; he was followed moments later by two more. There were now five in all, the entire group that had been in his yard earlier.

They remained gathered for some time, having a discussion of some sort. When they broke apart, a few minutes later, Marr, with one rider, turned back down the mountain. The remaining three split and disappeared once again into the rock and brush.

It was evident to Ben what was taking place. Marr and one man, probably Bibo

Sabine, were abandoning the search. The other three men would continue. They now were moving west across the slope of the mountain, a course that would eventually bring them to a dead end on the rim of the deep canyon. There was nothing to fear from them, unless he permitted himself to be seen and thus reveal his position. They could do nothing when they came to the canyon except turn back and retrace their trail.

Dunn lay back; his eyes turned upward to the cloudless arch overhead. In the arid, towering world atop Comanche Mountain, sound carried with startling clarity. He could easily hear the buckskin cropping contentedly at the grass; the far off moaning of a dove, the rapid clacking of an insect a hundred yards up the ridge. Turning that way, he saw motion, saw it freeze. He beheld a buck mule deer, with a wide spread of antlers, herding his harem of does. All were etched against a background of grays and greens.

He remained absolutely still, enjoying the sight. When the old buck did not again see anything of a suspicious nature, he sauntered on, trailed obediently by his mincing retinue. They soon were lost in the tall grass.

Dunn whiled away the remainder of the

afternoon, and, when it was nearly dark, he came off the ridge and headed back for his ranch. He knew there was little, if any chance of running into Marr's men at this late hour. They would have long ago given up the search.

He must find Laura and help her. That she had somehow managed to escape Marr was clear. Where could she have gone to hide? She was a stranger in the country and would know little of it. She must be somewhere between his own Box B holdings and Diamond X. It was the only area she had been through. And Marr seemed to believe she had come to his place. Wherever she was, she must be found. He was the only friend she had — the only one who could help her.

First he must have a gun. It would be foolish to begin a search without a weapon. One of Marr's riders, the one they called Harvey, had picked up his revolver when Ben had been compelled to drop it. There was no point in looking for it in the yard. But that was of no great consequence. The mate to it was in the footlocker in his house. There had been a time when he carried two guns.

He worked his way carefully through the brush and rock, and, when he drew near the buildings of the Box B, he halted within the thick brush that rimmed the yard. There was every chance that Marr had left men to keep an eye on the place. Still, he could see no horses, nor hear any suspicious sounds.

It was too quiet. And to believe that Marr had not set men to watch the ranch was foolhardy. He tied the buckskin well back in the brush, hoping he would not sense the nearness of his stable mates in the barn and give his presence away. Dunn began to work in closer.

He remembered the old rifle and a handful of shells he kept in the barn. He had placed them there at one time for use on coyotes and wolves which occasionally slink in from the mountain in search of a calf or other easy meal. He decided it was a better gamble to try for it than enter the house for the six-gun. Accordingly, he dropped back, circled wide, and came up to the barn on its blind side. It was a simple matter to crawl through the window and gain entrance.

Once inside, he paused to listen. He heard only the muted breathing of the horses, an occasional dry rasp as they changed positions and rubbed against the sides of their stalls. Dunn moved softly into the runway. He stayed close to the wall, where the shadows were deepest, made his way to the front of the barn. The rifle should be hanging on a peg just inside the door. The cartridges would be lying nearby on the wooden crosspiece that braced the studding.

He came to the end of the runway. He saw the rifle. It was on the opposite side. Moonlight striking through the open doorway, laid danger across his path. To get the rifle meant exposing himself to anyone who might be watching at that moment, either from the inside of the barn, or outside. But he needed the gun. He stepped boldly into the flood of light, moving quickly.

"Ben!"

The summons reached out of the darkness, caught him in stride. It was the voice of Laura Pope.

7

He hesitated only momentarily, then completed the distance to the rifle and ammunition. Casting a long look at the dark bulk of his house, he wheeled, swiftly recrossed the runway, and retreated into the darkness at the rear of the barn.

"Ben," Laura said again. "I'm over here."

He pivoted at the sound of her voice. It came from behind stacked sacks of grain in an unused stall. She rose to meet him.

"Didn't expect to find you here," he said. "Was about to start out and hunt."

"I came as soon as it was dark. I don't think anyone saw me."

"Anybody been around?"

"Three men. The one they call Pete and two others."

"That would be Frisco, with Harvey and Charlie. They would have stopped by for a look when they came off the mountain. How about Marr?"

"Haven't seen him since I left the ranch."

He walked back to the runway, to a position where he could see the yard and keep an eye on the house. Laura followed.

"You know Isaac Pope is dead?"

"Yes, I know," she replied in a toneless voice.

He turned, took her shoulders between his two hands. She was near the breaking point. "Everything's going to be all right now," he said. "You know they're accusing us of doing it?"

She looked up at him. "I didn't know about you. I'm sorry about it."

"We're both in on it. Marr and his bunch were here. Claims you and I framed the whole thing, that we're working together. He says we cooked up this daughter thing so you could inherit the Pope ranch. Then we killed Pope."

She brushed at her eyes. "It's unbelievable! It's all happened so fast —"

"You have any idea who might have killed Pope?"

"No, I haven't," she said. "When I saw him last, he was alive."

"This thing's going to be hard to clear up," Dunn said in a thoughtful voice. "Be tough to scrape up proof that will point to the real killer."

"I'm sorry I dragged you into it," Laura said. "Seems I've caused you nothing but trouble from the very start."

"Forget it," he replied. "You said I was a friend. I intend to prove it's true — maybe that I'm even more than just that."

She gave him no answer, only moved closer to him. After a time she asked, "What do we do next?"

"I've got to put you where you'll be safe," he said. "Think the best idea is to get you to Salt River. That's the nearest town where there's people and a hotel. And the marshal's got his office there. Marr's plan was to take us to him and make his charge of murder against us. If we can get there first and tell him our side of the story, maybe we'll have a good chance of clearing things up."

She stepped back from him. "But I have no proof to show him, no way to back up my story that Isaac Pope was my father. Wouldn't we be playing right into Marr's hands?"

Dunn frowned in the darkness. "That letter and the picture you told me about, they're still at the Pope place?"

"Yes," she said. "There was no time to get anything."

He considered that for a time. Then,

"How did you get here? You didn't walk all the way?"

"No, I had a horse. At least, I started with one. I was up and dressed early. I heard Marr and someone talking. It was right after they found my father dead. I listened and learned that they thought I had something to do with it and that they were coming to get me. I slipped out of a window. There were some horses tied up at the rail. I took one and got away before they realized it."

"They follow you?"

"Yes, but I had several minutes' start. They began to catch up and I pulled off into the brush and hid. My horse broke away after they passed and I had to go on, on foot. It wasn't far from here. Only two or three miles."

"That must have been about the time they rode in here," Dunn said. "Marr figured, when he missed you, that you probably came straight to me. I'm glad that you did."

He moved off toward the stalls where the horses rested. "I'll saddle a mount for you. My buckskin is waiting out there in the brush. We'll head for Salt River early as we can."

She was silent while he threw the gear on one of the bays. That finished, he again looked toward the house. "Have to get us

74

some grub. Full day's ride to the town. I haven't had anything since this morning and I expect you haven't either. Then we'll need some for the trail. Nothing to do but chance it."

"Chance what?"

"That none of Marr's bunch is hanging around, watching the place." He picked up the rifle, cracked its mechanism to check the chamber. There was a cartridge in place. "Stay here. Keep in the dark," he said and dropped back to the window through which he had previously made an entrance.

He leaped softly to the ground, paused a moment to listen. He heard nothing and crossed the length of the building. At its corner he went to his hands and knees, crawled swiftly along the fringe of brush to a point directly behind the ranch house. Again he waited a time. He heard no unusual sounds and, still crouched, he dashed across the open ground, gained the rear of the structure.

There was no possibility of entering through a back window, as he had done at the barn. All were too small. There was a side door to one of the rooms he had built on, but it was securely barred. It would be useless to attempt to force it. His one means was through the front.

He circled the house, keeping in the shadows of the brush, halted when he was in a position to see the door. It was clearly visible in the moon-flooded night, as was the open yard across which he would have to make his way. If anyone were watching the house, it would be impossible for a man to reach that door unnoticed.

The faint jingle of metal stiffened him. He raised up, listened intently. He heard then the dry creak of leather.

He sank down slowly, went to his belly. Flat on the ground, he considered what must be done. The sound had originated off to his right, not far away. Jack Marr had left a guard, just as Ben had suspected he might. Likely there was only one; with him out of the way, he could complete the necessary preparations for the trip to Salt River. Then Laura and he could be on the trail.

He worked his way silently off through the dark, making only a short distance at a time. It was a tedious process but finally he saw the horse, tethered to a small tree. The man was a short distance beyond it. He had settled down, his back against a stump. His head was dropped forward on his arms which were crossed upon his knees. He was sleeping soundly.

Dunn raised himself carefully, probed the

night for a second horse and another sentry. He could see no evidence of either. At that moment the horse got wind of him. He jerked his head up sharply. The clear jingle of bridle metal broke the silence. The sleeping man awoke with a start. He glanced about, saw Ben. He clawed at the pistol on his hip. Dunn moved in like a swiftly-descending shadow. He brought the rifle down in a short arc. It thudded against the man's head, and he collapsed without a sound.

Dunn knelt over him, rolled him to his back. It was the one they had called Harvey. Ben's fingers explored along his belt, found what he knew should be there — his own revolver. He slid it into his empty holster, looked more closely at the cowboy. He would be out for some time.

He wheeled, trotted back the route he had come, still cautious to stay in the dark areas. There was still the possibility that Marr had left two, or even three men to watch; he would take no greater risks than necessary. He reached the corner of the house, halted there for a time while he searched the brush beyond the moonlit yard. He could see nothing, and, delaying no longer, he crossed to the door and hurriedly let himself inside.

Immediately he began to gather the

needed items: his saddlebags; a canteen of water; coffee pot; a sack of coffee beans; bread; dried meat; two tins of peaches; a handful of potatoes. Stowing all but the container of water in the leather pouches, he went back to the door. All was quiet outside. He left quickly, still trusting only to the shadows, and returned to the barn.

Inside he found Laura waiting where he had left her. He threw the saddlebags across the horse he had selected for her, jammed the rifle into the boot.

"Marr left a man to watch the house. Could be there's another. We better get out of here fast."

"What happened? Did you have to —"

"Only a rap on the head. He'll be quiet for a spell, long enough for us to get going."

He backed the bay out the runway. "We'll have to use the door," he said. "No opening in the back of this barn big enough for a horse. If Harvey was the only man Marr left, we'll have no trouble. If there's another, we may have to run for it."

She said, "I understand."

"Mount up," he said, dropping back to assist her. "Then you'll be ready to ride if need be. My horse is behind the barn. I'll lead the way."

Laura settled herself in the saddle with no

78

comment. Dunn took the reins in his left hand, leaving the right free, and started for the doorway. They reached the opening. He halted briefly and then stepped out into the yard. There he again paused, half expecting to hear the crash of a gun, feel the smash of a bullet. There was only the distant murmurs of night birds in the trees.

He moved out again, walked fast. They gained the corner of the barn without incident, turned, passed along its length. A minute later they were within the safety of the brush. Either Marr had picketed only Harvey to watch, or else the others also were asleep.

They reached the buckskin, halted. Dunn took the saddlebags laid across the girl's horse, and fastened them securely to his own gear. He anchored the canteen to the horn. Finished, he glanced up at Laura. A shaft of silver moonlight cutting through the leaves of an overspreading tree fell across her face, pointing up its soft beauty. She was looking off into the night.

"Been a bad day for you," he said, stepping onto his horse.

"We'll travel for an hour or so and then stop. I know a spot where we can rest for a time and have a bite to eat."

8

In the stillness that followed his words, there was only the far away, lonely sound of a bird calling into the dark of night. He glanced at her, wondered if exhaustion had at last caught up with her, if she were asleep. She saw him turn and smiled wanly.

He reached out, took the reins of her horse into his hand. He touched the buckskin with spurs and they moved out immediately, the bay holding back a little but following, nevertheless.

They rode steadily for a lengthy hour, and then pulled into a small clearing that fronted a cave-like opening in the base of the mountain. Holding to her horse, Dunn swung down.

"We'll rest here until it's lighter. I'll make coffee."

Wearily, she twisted about. He helped her to the ground, and she walked to the edge of the hollow, gouged from the slope as though by some gigantic hand, and sat down. He secured the horses in the brush beyond the cleared area and returned, bringing with him the saddlebags and canteen. He built a small fire, placed the sooty pot, half-filled with water, over the flames. He began to rummage through the food he had provided.

"Be just a few minutes," he said to her. "And it won't be much, but it will do until we get to Salt River. Good cafe there. We'll have a real supper then."

She smiled at him, expressed her thanks. He turned to his chore. From the saddlebags he obtained some dried meat, several hard biscuits. He opened a tin of peaches, poured half into a cup for her. The coffee boiled up. He removed it from the fire, tipped back the lid. With a twig, he stirred down the froth. After it had settled, he poured two cups. He moved to her side, placed the food before her.

"Thank you," she murmured. "That coffee smells so good."

"One thing I guarantee," he grinned, "is that it's strong enough!"

Both were hungry and they ate steadily. The food was simple, but ample and filling. When they had finished, he replaced the cups and what was left of the food in the saddlebags and then returned to her. He settled down, rolled himself a cigarette.

"You didn't ask me what happened when I saw my father," she said. "Aren't you interested in knowing whether he accepted me as his daughter or not?"

He shook his head. "Reckon it didn't matter. If you are Laura Pope or someone else, it made no difference. I just figured you were and let it go at that."

"And if I had been an impostor, someone just trying to inherit the Pope ranch like that man Crawford thought?"

"Like I said, it would make no difference. I'm interested in you — not who you are."

She moved nearer to him, placed her hand on his arm. She leaned forward, kissed him lightly on the cheek.

"I'm afraid to think of how it might have been, if I hadn't met you," she said.

"Haven't done much good for you, yet," he said. "And we're not finished with this thing yet."

"I'm not afraid," she said. "Long as we're together, I know it will all work out."

He did not reply. She watched him draw deeply on his cigarette, then exhale slowly. She said, "Mr. Pope accepted me as his daughter before he was murdered. It was all settled. After he read my mother's letter and saw the picture likeness, he talked for a while. He had some papers in a box, near his bed. They seemed to prove something to him. Anyway, he was convinced. And just before I left his room, he mentioned a trunk in which he said there were some more pictures, tintypes. We were going to get them out today."

"That's fine," Dunn said. "I'm glad you were able to prove it to him — and that he got to see you before he was killed. After all, you are his only child. Did he talk with Marr after that?"

"I don't know. I expect he did."

"Marr would have to hear it from somebody. Likely it was Pope who told him. And that started things turning in Marr's head. He saw the Diamond X slipping out of his hands and he had to figure a way to hold it."

"Then he —"

Ben Dunn came up swiftly. He lifted his hand, closed off the girl's words. Back, somewhere along the route they had traveled, he had heard a noise: the distinct click of metal striking against rock.

Laura looked at him questionably. He shook his head, warned her to silence. It was hard to believe Marr, or any of his men, could have got onto their trail so quickly, and could have located them in the night. He thought of the fire he had built. There was the answer. Even a small one created a glow. They must have noticed it.

He drew his pistol, carefully scraped earth and trash over the now smouldering embers with the toe of his boot. He continued to listen, head cocked in the direction of the sound. There was nothing. It could have been a deer, he reasoned, or it might have been a horse and rider.

He glided silently to Laura. "Wait here," he whispered, "but if I'm not back in a couple of minutes, or if you hear sounds of trouble, get out of here fast. Ride straight west. I'll find you."

She nodded her understanding. He moved off at once into the silver-shot night. He kept to the dark shadows. It was slow going. He must avoid contact with brush that would scrape against him, set up a noise. He covered a hundred yards, and froze. The sound of a horse, blowing impatiently, reached him.

He remained rigid for a long minute, considering his best course of action. It was reasonable to think the sound had been made by a stray horse, one wandering about on the foot of Comanache Mountain. But he could assume nothing, take nothing for granted; he must know. He moved forward again with even greater care. He knew the approximate location of the animal now. That made it easier.

"That fire sure was around in here somewheres!"

Dunn hauled up short, blocked by the sudden, distinct declaration, as effectively as had he walked into a rock wall. It was Bibo Sabine's voice. The man could be no farther away than a wagon's length.

"Seems to me it was higher up."

Pete Frisco. Dunn wondered if there were more. He could see none of them. They were beyond a dense stand of cedar and scrub oak and on a lower level of the slope.

"What you say, Harvey? You figure they're higher up, or lower down?"

"My guess'd be they're up high. That's how come we seen the glow. And Dunn would want to be where he could see good."

"Play hell seein' much at night from anywhere," Sabine said.

"He'll be holed up, waitin' for daylight. Then him and the girl will move out. He'd pick a spot where he could watch from, sure enough."

"Reckon it don't matter," Frisco said. "Jack wants 'em both. We got to find 'em."

Dunn eased silently back into the darkness. He and Laura were on an almost direct line with the three riders. If they delayed longer, they would be discovered.

"Let's just keep ridin' the way we was," Sabine suggested. "But spread out like. And keep watchin' up the side of the mountain. Maybe we can spot that fire again."

Dunn pulled farther into the brush. He broke into a trot. He knew he was running the risk of tripping, of dislodging loose shale and creating a disturbance. But it could not be helped. He must get Laura out of the area fast. The three men would blunder down upon them in a very few minutes.

"You hear somethin?" Sabine's question came to him clearly. "Sounded like it was just ahead, somewheres in them bushes."

Dunn broke into the clearing. The noise of Sabine and the other men approaching now was plain in the hush. He halted, glanced about. Laura was not there. His saddlebags, the canteen and the coffee pot lay where he had left them. He snatched up the water container and the bags, ignored all else. Laura, likely, was with the horses. He plunged across the open ground for the thicket where he had left their mounts.

Only the buckskin remained. Laura, heeding his warning, had fled.

It was just as well. But he must be certain.

He moved to the buckskin, threw the saddlebags and canteen into place.

"Laura," he whispered into the darkness.

There was no reply. He stepped to the saddle, probed the dark shrubbery with anxious eyes. "Laura!" he repeated, raising his voice.

The night yielded no answer. He could delay no longer and there was no question the girl had gone. He moved out.

"Over there!"

Bibo Sabine's hoarse voice was like a sharp sword thrust through the darkness. "There he is — edge of that clearin'!"

A gun blast shattered the stillness. Ben heard the shriek of a bullet, the sudden pound of onrushing horses only yards away.

"Circle around!" Sabine yelled. "Cut him off 'fore he can get away!"

Dunn spun the buckskin about in a tight circle. He drove home his spurs. The horse plunged ahead, crashed through a low hedge of scrub oak, stumbled, caught himself and went on. Another gun smashed through the whirling confusion. Ben flung a glance to the clearing. Through the lacework of moonlight and shadows he saw the three riders converge. It was too dark to tell which was which; it did not matter.

He jerked the buckskin hard right, headed

downgrade. Instantly one of the cowboys fired. The bullet caromed off the trunk of a nearby pine tree, wailed into space. He swerved the buckskin to the left, driving hard, recklessly. The horse was racing madly through the night, plunging through brush, stumbling, leaping over fallen logs. His ears were laid flat, long neck extended.

"Keep after 'em! Keep 'em runnin'!"

Sabine's hoarse commands were like a crackling whip to the rear. He apparently thought Laura was with him, Dunn realized. He was thankful she was not. She could never have stayed on the saddle through such a nightmarish ride.

He was striking upgrade now, climbing the slope of Comanche Mountain. He could not continue for long. It was much too difficult for the buckskin. He was slowing down and, in so doing, Dunn realized he was presenting Sabine and the two riders with an easy target.

He sliced back immediately, not to the right again — that would have taken him in the direction he had been following — but to the left, thus doubling back. He reasoned that such a move would be unexpected by Marr's riders and it would also pull them off Laura who was somewhere further to the west.

Sabine was too close to be misled. He saw Ben change directions, snapped a quick shot. The bullet struck somewhere behind the saddle horn, ricocheted noisily into the forest. The sound gouged the buckskin's shattered nerves. He shied, came to a plunging, skidding halt, almost catapulting Dunn from his back.

Dunn jabbed at the confused animal's ribs mercilessly. The horse righted himself, cut straight down slope, headed directly for Sabine and the others. It was useless and too late to try and stop him. Dunn dragged out his own gun. Sabine was abruptly before him. He threw a bullet at the rider, saw that he had missed, and was carried on in a wild rush by his crazed horse.

Instantly the three men opened up at him. The night was suddenly filled with screaming lead, echoing blasts. Dunn, twisting and dodging to avoid being swept from the saddle by low-hanging branches and dragged to the ground by clawing brush, struggled to stay with the buckskin. Each second he expected to feel the searing shock of a bullet driving into his body.

The horse swerved to avoid a solid wall of brush. In the next instant he felt the buckskin quiver, stagger to one side. He had been hit. The horse reared, pawed the air frantically with his forelegs. He began to fall back, go down into the bushes.

Dunn leaped clear. He struck on all fours. He was up instantly, plunging off into the darkness. Behind him rose the shouts of Sabine, Frisco and Harvey. They had seen the buckskin go down, thought he was under the threshing animal. He did not look back to see if they had stopped. He rushed on down the steep grade, his long legs taking monstrous strides as momentum lent him speed. He was inviting disaster at every step. He fought to slow down, and maintain balance, but he was like a leaf caught in a blast of wind.

The crash of the riders through the brush was loud again. They had discovered he was not with the luckless buckskin and was again seeking escape. He slanted off to his left. If he could reach the big canyon, he might have a chance. In that wild and badly overgrown area there were many places where a man could hide.

He plunged recklessly on, speed unchecked. He tried to keep in the shadows, but there was little choice in direction on his part. He fought to stay out of the open where Sabine and the others could get a shot at his back.

"There he goes!"

It was Pete Frisco who yelled. Ben hurled himself to one side, sought to destroy any target he might be presenting. All three riders fired together, orange flashes marking their positions. They were close — too close to him.

Abruptly, right under his feet it seemed, the ragged edge of an arroyo yawned. It was impossible to check his headlong speed. He leaped, trusted to luck that the ravine was not too wide and that he would find safe footing on its far side. His boots hit the opposite wall. In that identical moment his body crashed into a small tree or bush of some sort, he did not know which. He felt himself hurled backwards. He clawed frantically to catch himself, failed, dropped back into the deep slash.

"Look out!" Bibo Sabine's warning came from directly overhead.

He struck the ground just as the three horses leaped over the arroyo, soared above him in a clatter of displaced gravel and rattling brush, then thundered on.

He lay still for several seconds, sucking for breath. He was flat on his back on the sandy floor of the ravine. He had been lucky. He was unhurt and the three riders, apparently having seen him leap, thought he had successfully cleared the arroyo and was still going, somewhere off in the darkness of the opposite side. They had not witnessed his fall.

He could not stay there. He realized that and struggled to his feet. When they did not again locate him, they would come back. He started down the arroyo at a trot, electing to stay within its depth. It was not hard going but he was still short of breath from the hard run and the fall. The ravine should lead him to the canyon, he figured. Once there his chances of survival would be greatly improved.

He rounded a sharp curve in the arroyo. The dark, indefinite outline of something — of a horse, slowed his steps. It was standing broadside in the narrow slash. A strange sort of dread, an emotion unfamiliar to Dunn, clutched at his throat. It was the bay he had provided for Laura. Where was she? What had happened?

He hurried to the patient animal which swung his long head about, watched him run up with stolid indifference. The girl was not nearby. He looked about thoroughly. He took the bay's reins, continued on for another ten yards. Then he saw her. She lay at the foot of the ravine's steep bank. She had not been as fortunate as he when her horse attempted to clear the arroyo.

He rushed to her, knelt beside her still, crumpled form. He turned her over gently, peered down into the pale oval of her face. A terrible fear gripped him. She looked so calm, so white. He lowered his head, placed his ear to her lips. A feeling of relief slipped through him. She was breathing. He placed his arm under her shoulders, raised her slightly. An ugly bruise was beginning to darken the side of her head, just above the left cheekbone. A ragged, raw scratch traced down her neck where an out-thrusting branch had clawed her.

He glanced hurriedly around. He needed water for her. But there was no spring nearby, and the canteen was on the saddle of his buckskin. He began to chafe her wrists with brisk, hard motions. She stirred in the cradle of his arm. Her lids fluttered, opened. Her eyes at first filled with alarm and then calmed as she recognized him.

"Oh, Ben —"

He laid a finger across her lips, silenced her. "Quiet, Marr's bunch is around close. We can't make any noise. Are you hurt?"

She stirred in his arm. "I don't think so. My shoulder feels a little numb."

"You've got a bad bruise on your face, too. How did it happen?"

She explored the side of her head gingerly.

"I don't exactly know. One minute I was riding, heading west like you told me to. Next thing I was sailing through the air."

That accounted for the bay coming through unhurt. He had simply stopped short when he saw the arroyo. Laura had been thrown over his head. It was fortunate she had struck mostly on the soft sand, not higher up against the ragged-edged rocks and stiff brush.

"Think you can ride?" he asked. "We've got to get away from here. Sabine and his bunch will find us if we stay."

She said, "I'll manage. Was that who it was back there?"

"Sabine, Frisco and the one they call Harvey."

He got to his feet, helped her rise. They stood there for a short time, she testing her strength. Dunn listening into the night. He thought he could hear Sabine and the others but he was not sure. In any event, he could take no chances.

He wheeled to the bay, led him up to her. He helped her swing into the saddle. She looked about questioningly.

"Where's your horse?"

"Back on the mountain," he said. "Stopped a bullet. I'll lead you out of this canyon, then we'll have to ride double."

"Are we still going to Salt River?"

"Not much chance now," he said and moved out ahead of the bay. "This horse would never make it, carrying us both. And we've got no water or grub."

She considered his words for a time. "Then what can we do?"

The trail was rough, indistinct. Dunn was forced to go carefully. He said, "Some people by the name of Loveless have a place a few miles farther on. They're friends of mine. We'll head there. I've been thinking about that idea I had of going to the marshal. Could be it wasn't so good. Seems I recall that Marr and him were pretty close friends. Without anything to back up our story, we might have a hard time making him see things our way."

"Can the Lovelesses help us?"

"They'll do all they can, but Abner is an old man. Sabine roughed him up some a few days ago. I don't want to get them too mixed up in this, because it could bring them a lot of trouble."

Laura said, "I see."

They were approaching the end of the arroyo. Here it would be necessary to climb out onto nearly level land.

He led the bay, with Laura clinging tightly to the saddle horn as her mount scrambled up the last few feet of the trail, on to a fairly level meadow. He halted there, allowed the horse to recover himself while he turned his attention to their back trail. There were no signs of Marr's men but he could not be entirely sure. Night masked all movement, even at short distance. Still, it worked both ways; if he could not see them, they would have no better luck spotting Laura and him.

He swung up behind the girl, onto the bay. The horse moved off, walked slowly through the short grass. The animal was tired, and the extra burden of Dunn was unwelcome. He held up, reluctant to proceed. Dunn goaded him gently with his spurs and finally, the bay continued.

Laura leaned back, relaxed in the circle of his arms. "I'll be so thankful when this is all over with," she murmured.

"It won't be long," he answered.

9

The Loveless place was dark, as he expected it would be. It was still an hour or more until daylight and the elderly couple would yet be asleep.

He rode into the small, clean-swept yard, headed the weary bay towards the corral behind the house. Laura had given in to exhaustion, had sagged against him, and dozed for the last several miles. When he halted the horse, she awakened with a start.

"Where are we?"

"At Abner's," he said, dropping off the bay. He extended his hands to help her dismount. The night had turned chilly and she was shivering.

"Be just a minute," he said. "Got to put this horse up. He's had a hard time of it. I'll fix some coffee when we get inside."

She nodded her understanding, stepped back and watched while he loosed the bay's saddle and removed it and the bridle. The horse headed wearily into the square of axed logs, began at once to eat a pile of hay thrown into one corner. Dunn returned and with Laura entered the house.

It was little more than a shack, constructed mostly of castoff lumber, tar paper, mud bricks, and logs. It consisted of one large room, which served as kitchen, dining area, and living room. Sleeping quarters for the couple was a separate section built off one end. Once inside, Dunn stepped softly across the central room and quietly closed the slab door that divided the two.

"No use waking them up," he said in a low whisper. He pointed to a cowhide chair. "Sit down and rest. I'll get the stove going."

Laura did as he directed and he turned to the cast-iron range. With little noise, he got a fire going. Once that was done he took the granite coffee pot, clean as the day it was new, filled it from the nearby bucket and sat it on the steadily heating surface of the range.

"Feels so good," Laura said in a thankful voice. She leaned forward, extended her hands, palms outward, to the stove. "I'll never get used to this country! So hot in the day, yet it turns so bitter at night."

He nodded. "Way of the desert." He squatted on his heels, began to roll a cigarette, doing it in the quick deft way of a man who had performed the task a thousand times over. He lit the slim cylinder, sucked the smoke deep into his lungs.

She watched him taking his ease for a time. There was a calmness about him now, a quiet, relaxed quality to his sun-browned features that changed him, turned him into a different person. It was as if, within four walls, the world was far removed from his conscious self and there were no troubles, no threats, no promises of violence.

The water in the pot began to rumble, rattle the lid of the container. He rose, helped himself to a handful of already-ground coffee, dumped it into the pot. The liquid boiled up immediately, and he pushed the granite utensil to the cooler side of the stove to simmer. He took two cups, dropped the oven door, improvising a convenient table, and placed them upon it. The room had grown warm and cheery.

He allowed the coffee to murmur for a bit. When he decided it was ready, he filled the cups. "This will hold us until the Lovelesses get up." he said. "Then we'll have some breakfast."

He went back to his haunches before the open oven, sipped at the black, steaming drink with relish. Laura finished her own portion, placed the cup aside on the edge of the stove. Automatically, he reached for the granite pot.

She said, "Not just now."

He refilled his own, settled back again. She leaned toward him.

"What do you plan to do next, Ben?"

At her question he glanced up. "I want you to stay here with Abner and Hopeful. I'm going over to Diamond X and see what I can find out."

"Won't that be taking a big chance? Marr is sure to have everything watched."

Dunn shrugged. "No other answer that I can see. I've got to clear you, and myself, of that murder charge."

"What can you expect to learn there?"

"Several things. I want to talk to some of the old hands that worked for Pope. Mainly, though, I mean to get those things you mentioned, the ones that prove you are Isaac Pope's daughter. We've got to have them."

"They will be in the house, in his room, if they haven't been moved. Shouldn't I go with you and help?"

He said, "Too dangerous," and ended the subject.

There was a sound behind them. They turned. Abner Loveless, clad in a long, white nightgown, his thin hair askew, stood in the doorway of the bedroom. He saw Laura and hastily withdrew until only his head was visible.

"Thought I heard somethin' out here," he declared. "When'd you come, Ben?"

"Hour or so ago. This is Laura Pope, Isaac's daughter."

"Pleased to meet you," the old man said. He disappeared from sight. "Hopeful, get up!" he shouted into the bedroom. "We got us some company."

In a short time the old couple were dressed and gathered before the stove. Dunn poured them coffee, made the introductions complete. When that was done, Hopeful Loveless, a sweet-faced woman with iron-gray hair, busied herself at her food stores.

" 'Spect you're mighty hungry. I'll get breakfast to cooking."

"I'll help," Laura volunteered and moved to her side.

Abner Loveless placed his attention on Dunn. "Reckon you had a reason for comin' here in the middle of the night. Anything I can do to help?"

Ben said, "Pope was killed last night."

"Kilt?" Loveless echoed, astonished. "Who by?"

"Marr is trying to put it on Laura and me. He's telling it around that we cooked up the deal so we could get our hands on the Diamond X."

Abner was silent for a long minute. Dunn read the question that was in his mind. "She is Pope's daughter. She showed him proof and he accepted her before he was killed. I figure Jack Marr had a hand in it. He didn't want to lose out, so he got Pope out of the way before the old man could make it known that his daughter had come back."

"Then Jack started gunnin' for you two, figurin' he'd have to get you out of the way."

"He's got to hang it on somebody. Laura was the natural one. Then, me, too, because I helped her a little. We've been dodging Sabine and Frisco and the one they call Harvey all yesterday and last night."

"Where they now?"

"Don't know exactly. Gave them the slip back on the mountain. They could have gone back to Pope's."

"Nope, they'll still be lookin'. What you figure to do next?"

"Like to leave Laura here with you. I'm riding over to Pope's and see what's going on and try to get my hands on that proof Laura needs before Jack destroys it."

"Be takin' quite a chance," Loveless said.

"How you figure to get the stuff?"

"Something I don't know yet. Cross that creek when I get to it."

"Shame there ain't some law around here a man could turn to," Loveless muttered.

Laura heard his comment, came about. "I thought there was a marshal in Salt River!"

"A town marshal, ma'am," Abner explained. "He's got no authority outside Salt River, unless it's Jack Marr that's talkin' to him. Then he's as big as a United States Marshal."

She faced Ben Dunn. "But if he —"

"Don't worry about it," he said. "We get the proof we need, we'll convince him. But we've got to do it before Marr talks to him."

"What about the murder charge?"

Dunn shook his head. "Something I haven't figured out yet. Hope to get some idea of what happened when I get to Pope's. There's a few of the old hands still there that don't take much to Jack and his gun toughs. Might learn a few things from them."

"If you can get to them to talk," Loveless amended.

"Something I've got to manage, somehow."

The meal was ready shortly after that. They gathered around the small table and ate in silence. When it was over, Dunn arose.

"Best I get started. Like to borrow one of your horses, Abner. That bay of mine is about run out."

"Sure," the old puncher said. "I'll help you saddle up."

Ben turned to Laura. "Just wait here for me. It'll take most of the day, but I'll be back. You can figure on that."

She said, "All right."

"If anybody shows up, stay out of sight, no matter who it is. Don't want anybody carrying word to Marr or any of his bunch about there being a girl here. They would know right quick who it is."

Again she said, "All right." She moved a step nearer to him, looked up into his still face. "This is going to be dangerous for you, Ben. I'm not sure I want you to go. I'm not sure now that it's worth it. Isn't there some other way it can be done?"

"Only way I know," he said. "Don't fret about me. I've lived these many years, I figure to keep on living a few more."

"You must — for my sake," she said softly. "Good-by."

"Good-by," he replied and followed Abner Loveless out into the breaking dawn.

10

Ben Dunn lay on the top of the butte and studied the Pope ranch. The sun climbed steadily toward its midday peak, but activity below, for some obscure reason, seemed at a standstill. There were a number of horses, saddled and ready for use, waiting in the corral behind the bunkhouse. No one went near them. He saw three men emerge from their quarters, cross the yard to the main house. They entered only to reappear minutes later and stroll aimlessly to the barn and back. It was as though a holiday from all labor had been declared at the Diamond X.

This both mystified and dismayed Ben Dunn. To get the proof Laura needed to establish her claim and to search for facts that would enable him to clear them both of the murder charge, he had to get inside the ranch house. To accomplish that he had to wait until Jack Marr and his riders pulled out to go about the daily affairs. Today, however, something was amiss. Neither they, nor any of the older hands were making any move to depart.

He lay sprawled full length on the rim of the lava butte and puzzled over the matter. It was while he was thus engrossed that he caught the sounds of an approaching horse. It came from the east, from the general direction of Comanche Mountain. He threw a quick glance to his own mount, picketed a dozen yards down the slope. Growth along the black, ragged formation was scant. There was little he could do to conceal the animal's presence from anyone arriving on that side.

But he could provide himself with some degree of cover. He rolled swiftly to a nearby clump of stringy greasewood. It made a poor screen, but it would afford him the chance to see who the oncoming rider might be.

It was Laura Pope.

Her name leaped from his lips when her worn horse broke out of a narrow arroyo, pulled up onto the top of the butte. She halted instantly. A wave of fear washed over her features when she heard his exclamation, but it disappeared at once when she recognized him. She smiled.

"Stay there," he called.

He worked his way back from the edge of the butte until he reached a point where he would not be seen by anyone at the ranch; and then rising, he hurried to her.

She was near exhaustion. He reached for her and lifted her from the saddle, noting as he did so that she was riding a Diamond X horse. He carried her to a shallow basin where a twisted juniper had managed to grow. He laid her in its dappled shade.

"I'm so glad I found you," she said. "I didn't think it was so far."

He dropped back to his horse, obtained his canteen. Returning, he poured a little of the tepid water between her lips. He wet his fingers and dampened her forehead and temples.

She smiled up at him. "I feel better."

She had pulled an old, faded pair of Abner's denims over her dress and had covered her shoulders with one of his light jackets. The hat she wore to protect her head from the driving sun was one of Hopeful's. He set aside the canteen.

"What happened back at the Loveless place? Why did you come here?"

"It was those men who were after us. Sabine and the other two. They came an hour or so after you had left. We saw them in time, and Abner hid me out in a shed, after furnishing me with these clothes. He was afraid they would search the place and told me, if they did, I was to leave at once.

"We arranged a signal and he showed me the trail I was to take that would lead me to you, or where he figured you would be. They came, tied their horses to the corral only a few feet from where I was hiding. When Abner gave me the signal, I took the first horse I could get to — one of theirs — and lit out."

Dunn thought for a few moments. "I'm glad you managed to get away," he said, finally. "Did you hear any shooting back at Abner's?"

"No, but when I looked back later I saw a lot of smoke. I guess they burned down their house."

Dunn stared off into the east. His jaw was set to grim, hard lines. "If they hurt those people," he said in a voice so low she could scarcely hear, "they'll answer to me. I've tried to avoid any bloodshed, but they'll have it if they've done anything bad to the Lovelesses."

"I thought later, when I was coming here, that maybe I should have stayed. Perhaps I could have helped."

He shook his head. "No. Abner was right.

Finding you there would have made things worse. The lucky part is that you found me."

"Abner pointed to a gap in the hills. Said you would be going into it. Is the ranch near here?"

"Just below this butte," he said. "I've been watching but still haven't figured out how to get inside the house. Seems everybody's hanging around close."

Laura came to a sitting position. "Don't try it, Ben," she said earnestly. "After you left this morning, I was sorry I let you go. I don't care about the Diamond X anymore. Let Jack Marr have it. I realized that all that mattered to me is you."

He glanced at her briefly. His arm went quickly about her, and he drew her swiftly to him. "Hearing you say that means a lot to me, everything, in fact. But I wouldn't let myself hope too much. Pretty poor sort of a life is all I can offer you."

"All I want. Just the two of us, together — to be left in peace."

He was silent for a time. Then, "Wish it could be that easy. You forget Marr. He'll never let it lie. We're a threat to him, long as we're alive."

"Why?" she wondered, drawing back from him. "If I give up my claim on the Diamond X, why wouldn't he forget about us?"

"Man like him has to be sure of his ground. He could never be. And then there's the death of your father to be accounted for. He's branded us as the killers. We have to clear that up, for our own sake."

"Can't we just go away, leave this country and start over somewhere else where nobody knows us?"

"Running away won't be the answer," he said. "I learned that a long time ago."

"What can we do then? You can't fight them all!"

"We've got to get inside the house," he replied. "We need the proof that will back your claim to being Isaac Pope's daughter. That will knock Marr's contention that you are an imposter. When that's done it'll be a big step toward making him eat that murder charge."

"That proof won't be hard to find," she said, "if Marr hasn't already destroyed it. Some of it he may not have known about. The tintypes my father said were in a trunk, for instance. And there was that box of papers by the bed."

"Only way we're going to know for sure about anything, is to get inside the house and look. You feel all right now?"

She nodded. "What do we do next?"

"Go back to the rim and watch the ranch.

Soon as Marr and his bunch leave, we'll go down. We'll have to take a chance on the regular help."

They crawled back to the lip of the butte, looked down upon the Pope buildings. They were scarcely settled when the side door opened and a man came out. He walked quickly to the barn and disappeared into it for a short time. He reappeared driving a light wagon. He guided it to the front of the house and halted.

Minutes later several men walked out onto the gallery, took up positions in the yard beyond the vehicle. Immediately they were followed by six others carrying a coffin between them. As they moved to the wagon, slid the elongated box onto its bed, Dunn realized why there had been no activity around the ranch during the early hours; they were holding a funeral for Isaac Pope.

More persons came from the house, lined up in pairs behind the wagon. Other than the man who appeared to be a minister, it looked as though no outsiders and only those who worked for the Diamond X were attending the burial.

The procession began, headed out across the yard for the small, family cemetery on a slight rise of ground a half mile distant. Ben felt Laura stir at his side. He placed his hands upon hers.

"I know I should be sad," she said. "He was my father. But I never knew him. I remember seeing him only that once, when I came the other day."

"Nobody would expect more of you," Dunn assured her. "I didn't know him either. Met him only a couple of times. He was a hard man, tough as they come, but he was honest and he was fair. Expect that's as good a recommendation as any man could have."

The long cortege was fully strung out by then. It appeared all of Diamond X's hands were in it, even the Mexican cook who walked along by herself.

"This is going to be our chance," Dunn said. "They'll be gone an hour, at least. Gives us time to reach the house, find the things we need and get out."

She said, "I'm ready when you are."

"Be better if you wait here. No use for you to take any risk."

"No, I want to be with you, Ben. Besides, I know where everything is. We can save time if I go. How do we get off this bluff?"

He grinned at her. She could be determined when she wished. He pointed off to their left. "There's a break in the butte a couple of hundred yards. We can ride down, cross over and come in behind the ranch house. That patch of trees will be a good place to leave the horses."

She began to withdraw from the rim. "We should get started. I'd hate to get trapped inside the house."

11

It required no more than a quarter-hour to descend from the butte and reach the house. They hid their horses in the trees, crossed quickly to the front door of the low, rambling structure and let themselves in. It would be better to use that particular entrance, Dunn reasoned; for, if there were any who had not joined the cortege, they most likely would be somewhere in the rear of the building.

Once inside, he locked the door, and secured it behind them. The house was hot, stuffy, and heavy with a silence that was at once oppressive. They stood quietly and listened for any sounds that would indicate there were others about, but heard nothing.

Dunn said, "Expect we'd better get busy. We'll try Pope's room first."

They crossed the cluttered parlor, went down the hallway to where he had last seen Isaac Pope alive. The door was closed. He turned the knob softly, pushed the panel wide. The rancher's sleeping quarters were just as he had last seen them, with the exception of the now empty bed.

"That box you mentioned — where was it?"

Laura said, "In the top drawer of that washstand," and pointed to the dark varnished piece of furniture against the wall.

Dunn stepped to it, pulled open the designated drawer. It was empty. Quickly, he went through the rest. Except for some odds and ends of clothing, there was nothing of interest. He turned then to the bed itself, gave it a thorough search. There was no box. They went through the remainder of the room, found nothing. It was evident that the metal container Laura had seen Isaac Pope refer to, had been removed.

"Where did you leave your bag?" Dunn asked.

She turned about immediately, led the way to the bedroom she had used. A complete examination of it revealed that her small carpetbag, with its papers, was also missing. In the deathly-quiet house, they paused.

"It's no use," she said in a falling voice. "Jack has already taken care of everything."

Dunn shrugged. He crossed to a window

where he could look out onto the yard. He looked to the north, to the direction in which the funeral procession had disappeared. There was no one in sight. He pivoted slowly to Laura.

"Did Pope have an office or a room where he kept his records? Might be a desk there. And that trunk."

"I don't know," she answered. "There are several more rooms down that hall. One that Marr used."

They started along the corridor. At the first door, Dunn halted. He opened the darkly-stained panel. It was another bedroom. He went through it hurriedly, found nothing of interest.

"Marr's room," he said, rejoining Laura in the hall. "Hardly expect to find any of the things we're looking for in there. He would have hid them some other place."

They moved on to the next door. It proved to be a storage closet containing only bedding. There was one more opening in the corridor before it turned to a right angle and led to the rear of the house.

"This should be it," Dunn said and reached for the knob.

Somewhere a door slammed. Ben's hand, resting on the round contour of the handle, froze. At his shoulder, Laura drew up sharply. A gasp escaped her lips.

"Somebody is here!" she whispered in a strained voice.

He frowned, cautioned her to silence. Touching her lightly on the arm, he motioned for her to remain where she stood. He glided off then into the short stretch of hallway to his right, which, if he were guessing right, led to the dining quarters and the kitchen. He could not tell where the sound of the closing door had come from; he was certain it had not been in the front of the house.

The hall led out into the mess hall, as he had anticipated. He halted there in the open doorway, glanced about. The room was deserted. Through a bank of windows on the opposite side he could look into the yard, see the rear of the bunkhouse, the front of the barn. There was no one in sight. He brought his attention back to the dining area. To his left, at the end of the narrow room, was a door. He walked quickly to it, opened it softly, slowly. It was the kitchen. It, too, was forsaken.

Puzzled, he remained there, alert, listening. He heard only the distant, raucous scolding of a crow in the field beyond the barn. But a door had slammed — somewhere. He became aware of the fleeting moments. He could waste no more time searching for it; they would just have to gamble that the sound had come from outside, from one of the other buildings. He wheeled, retraced his steps to Laura. To her questioning glance, he shook his head.

"Somewhere in the yard, I reckon."

He opened the door before them. It was Isaac Pope's office, or what served for such. A huge, roll-top desk stood against one wall. Near it was a metal-bound, domed lid trunk which showed evidence of much usage. Ben went straight to it, Laura close at his side.

"He said something about pictures," she recalled.

Dunn immediately began to delve through it. After a time he straightened up. In his hands was a large, family Bible. He opened it, quickly read the finely-scripted words on the first sheet.

"The record," he said. "Shows here there was a daughter. Now all we need is something to prove you are that daughter."

With Laura peering over his shoulder, he hastily leafed through the thick book, came finally to several pages in the back into which had been inserted, in squares and ovals provided for such, a number of tintype photographs.

"Here it is," he announced. "Here's what

we need."

There was the wedding picture of Pope and the woman that was his wife.

"My mother," Laura murmured.

Below it was a date. There were two other likenesses of persons unknown and then one of a small child with flowing, dark curls and large eyes.

"That must be you," he said.

On the next page they found more of what they needed. There was a picture of Pope with his wife and their small daughter; one of Pope holding Laura on his knee, a third of her in the arms of her mother.

"That's the picture I have — or had; the one my mother gave me," Laura exclaimed. "Or rather, one just like it. That should be all we need to show the marshal."

Dunn said, "Maybe. We still have to prove to the marshal that you're the same girl."

"But the picture I have," Laura began and then faltered. "I forgot. It was in my bag."

"Exactly. We've got to find that bag. With the picture you have and the letter your mother wrote, we've got this thing licked."

He turned to Pope's desk, went through each pigeonhole and drawer, came up with nothing of value. "Let's take a look through the parlor," he said, and went back into the hallway. "Hardly a place where Marr would hide something, but it's our last bet."

They fell to the task at once, systematically checked every drawer, every shelf, all possible places. Eventually they gave it up.

"Either it isn't hidden inside the house or Marr has destroyed it," Dunn said.

Laura, her face solemn, said, "Could it be in the bunkhouse?"

Ben considered that. "Don't think so. Like the kitchen and the mess hall, I don't think he'd risk hiding it there. Too much chance of someone else finding it."

She moved up to him. "What can we do, Ben?"

He put his arm around her. "Don't worry, we're not licked yet. It's possible he's got it with him, carrying it in his saddlebags and waiting for a good moment to get rid of it." He stopped, added, "Wonder if we've got time to check in the barn, have a look at Marr's gear?"

He stepped away abruptly, glanced out the window. "Too late," he said. "They're coming back. We've got to get out of here."

Laura ran to his side. Several men were just beginning the descent of the low rise to the north. Others, strung out irregularly, trailed them. Ben picked up the Bible, tucked it under his arm.

"We've got this much, anyway. And it

might do the trick."

"But the one who did it — who killed my father — we haven't been able to find out anything about that!"

"That will have to come later."

There was the sudden drum of trotting horses outside in the yard. Dunn wheeled, threw his attention to that point.

"Who is it?" Laura asked, pressing close to him.

"Sabine," he answered, "with Frisco and Harvey. Guess they're just getting back from the Loveless place. That's one of Abner's horses Frisco is riding."

"Someone else is coming," Laura said. "Another man."

Dunn bent down to follow her direction, looked under the partly-drawn shade. Sabine and the two riders with him had stopped and awaited the newcomer. Dunn, suddenly tense, straightened up slowly.

Laura saw the change sweep over him. She said, "Who is it? Do you know him?"

He did not immediately answer. Then, "I know him," he said in a quiet voice. "That's Jay Greavey."

12

"Greavey!"

Laura Pope echoed the name as though it were the foreboding of doomsday. She clutched at Dunn's arm. "He's that man — that killer — you've been expecting to come!"

He did not answer. For him, that moment was like taking a long step back into the years that had gone. In those past few days he had been a different man: one living in a newly-born world in which there had been no shadows; one for whom there had been only the present and the future. His thoughts had centered on Laura, on what lay ahead for them. Now, suddenly, in the shape of an almost frail-looking man with sloped shoulders, a narrow face and flat, colorless eyes, the old world he had left behind once again possessed him.

His hand dropped to the gun at his hip, touched its smooth, worn butt. A coolness enveloped him, seeped into his long body, steadied his nerves. He threw a glance to the ridge. Marr and the other Diamond X people were in sight. Their advance was slow but they would not be long in reaching the yard. He calculated the risk; with three of Marr's men already at hand and the remainder only a short distance away, he would have no chance, even if he were to down Greavey at first clash. Besides, there was Laura to consider.

Through the window he heard Bibo Sabine say, "You lookin' for somebody, mister?"

Greavey said, "I am. Man by the name of Dunn. Heard he was living around in these parts. He work for this outfit?"

"Who's askin'?" Sabine's words were blunt, too blunt.

"Don't see as that's any of your business. But the name happens to be Greavey. Dunn here?"

Sabine shook his head. "Don't work here but I reckon I know him, all right. Better you wait for the boss. That's him comin' over there."

The gunman astride a tall sorrel, swung his narrow visage toward the ridge at which Sabine pointed. The horse was a nervous animal and continually fiddled his feet, backed and shied. Greavey jerked at the reins. "Dang horse is just new broke. What's been going on? A burying?"

"Just that," Sabine said. "This here Dunn you're talkin' about, stuck a knife in the owner of this ranch. If you're a friend of his'n —"

"I'm not," Greavey said, shortly.

"Ben," Laura broke into Dunn's consciousness. "What are we going to do?"

Her question brought an awareness of their immediate peril. He wheeled about. "We're getting out of here," he said and started across the room.

There was no escape through the front door nor out of the kitchen. With Laura at his heels, he moved down the hallway, entered Pope's quarters. He crossed the small room, quickly to one of the windows, raised it fully. The screen was nailed shut. He whipped out his knife, slashed the light, wire mesh.

"Quick," he said to the girl.

He helped her through the opening, followed himself. He closed the window but there was nothing he could do about the sagging screen. It did not matter too much. They were on the side of the house, opposite to the yard.

They broke into a run, crossed the open

ground to where their horses waited. He helped Laura to the saddle and then swung up himself.

"Keep to the brush," he said, pulling the bay around. "At least until we've put a little distance between us and the house. Then we'll make a run for the hills."

She signified her understanding, dropped in behind him. They moved out, holding their mounts to a walk. Dunn, one hand impeded by the Pope family Bible, twisted about, secured the book to his saddle with the leather strips provided for such purpose. Likely he would be needing both hands before the hour was over.

The narrow band of green cover began to thin out, resolve itself into short clumps of brush. At its end, Dunn halted. He turned about, looked toward the Pope ranch. Marr and the others had returned. He could not see the man himself, but the others were visible, moving around in that area behind the ranch house and in front of the barn and corral. Four riders waited in the saddle, apparently for Marr. Ben was not certain but he thought one was Greavey.

He brought his attention back to their own present situation. Ahead lay a long mile of almost smooth, barren country before they could reach the first outcropping of trees and brush that trickled down from the mountain. To their right, the lava buttes were an equal distance away, offering even less protection. He considered for a time, came to a decision.

"Can't stay here. We'll try for those trees straight ahead." Laura smiled. If she were aware of the danger that lay ahead of them, when they broke out into the open, she did not show it.

"Get in front of me," he said, and pulled off to one side. "We may make it without being separated, but, if we do, ride straight up the side of the mountain."

"If we get separated —" she began, haltingly.

"Don't stop. Try to get as far up the slope as you can. I'll find you. Ready?"

"Ready," she said and pushed on by him.

Her horse, or that of Pete Frisco, was tired. He wouldn't go far at a fast pace, Dunn saw. But they had no choice. And it was wiser to keep the better mount under him; if it became necessary, he could draw Marr and his riders off, allow Laura to escape.

Detection came quickly, even sooner than he had anticipated. They were no more than a hundred yards away from cover when he looked back, saw a half a dozen riders streaming out of the yard in pursuit. He glanced ahead. It was a long way to the trees, but, barring any accident, they would make it. Their lead on the Diamond X riders was of sufficient enough length to make it possible.

He swung his attention back to the riders again. Was Jay Greavey with them? He wondered, but at such distance he could not tell.

It was a close race, nearer than he had thought it would be. They reached the first scatter of brush and trees with Marr and the others little more than a hundred yards behind. He pulled up to Laura's side.

"Keep going!" he shouted. "I'll cut off, try to lead them away."

He did not wait for her to answer, simply veered his horse sharp left, heading into the steadily thickening forest, He heard a yell go up as he purposely exposed himself, knew at once they had risen to the bait. He cast a glance to the direction in which Laura had gone. She was already out of sight, swallowed up by the maze of rock and green growth.

He let the bay have his head, allowed him to rush on down the lanes between the pines and other trees. Guns opened up a short time later, but he heard no droning of bullets and guessed the men were shooting wild, hoping only to get lucky.

The forest grew more dense, began to slow the horse down considerably. Rocks and huge boulders were becoming more plentiful. Dunn realized he was driving into the heart of a rough area, a place where once a massive slide had occurred. This suited him well.

At the first opportunity, at a narrow ravine, he cut to his right, doubled back at a slight climb. He reached a small pocket in the rain-washed rocks, halted. There he was effectively screened from the lower level by piles of rock. He remained still, listening. In only moments he heard the thunder of Marr and his riders hurrying by. They had passed up the rugged slide area, guessing that he would continue on through the easier-traveled forest.

Satisfied with the turn of the chase, he put the bay into motion, struck out for the higher slopes of the mountain. He would find Laura; they would remain in hiding until Marr tired of the hunt and gave it up. They could then decide what next was to be done.

He located the girl an hour later.

Moving silently through the trees, on a higher plane where pine needles and oak leaves cushioned the floor of the forest, he saw first a patch of her dress which was exposed beneath the jacket she wore. He headed for it. Rounding a thick stand of brush, he came upon her sitting on a fallen log at the edge of an arroyo. Pete Frisco's horse, near exhaustion, stood a few yards away, head down, legs spread in the way of a spent animal.

She sprang to her feet as he came up, greeted him with a glad, relieved smile. "I heard all that shooting. I was afraid —"

"They didn't see me," he explained and swung down. "They were just shooting wild, hoping they'd make a hit. Are you all right?"

She moved up to him, put herself in the circle of his arms. "I'm fine," she murmured. "And I'm glad you're all right. When we're apart, I worry so. I'm always afraid I won't see you again . . ."

"Just stand easy!" a voice from the brush ordered. "My gun's on you, Dunn."

Ben stiffened. Greavey's voice! He felt Laura go tense against his body and begin to tremble. He swore inwardly. He had misjudged the gunman. Greavey had been smart enough to keep his eyes on Laura, knowing that Dunn would return to her if he managed to elude Marr.

Grim-faced, he watched Greavey ride

from the brush. The big sorrel stepped gingerly through the rocks and low brush.

"Get away from him, lady."

Ben pushed Laura to one side, until she was an arm's length away. She was staring at the gunman with a sort of fascination, her eyes spread wide with fear and horror. Dunn felt Greavey's empty gaze upon him, hard-cored and drilling.

"Been a long time," the gunman said in his soft, flat voice. "You sure dropped out of sight good." He jerked savagely at his reins, sought to settle down the nervous sorrel.

Dunn made no answer to his comments, simply rode out the long, terrible moments. That Greavey would give him his chance to use his own gun, of that he was certain. But that would come later, after Greavey played his game of cat and mouse. It was the way of gunslingers.

"Rode myself across this country half a dozen times. Never could find you. You been hiding in a hole?"

"Not hardly," Dunn said. "Got a ranch of my own now. Been there ever since I quit riding. Reckon you never came this way."

"Guess that's the truth," Greavey said. "Figured you'd be over Texas way." He paused to check the sorrel which was attempting to wheel completely around. He halted the horse. "Heard about you in Santa Fe. Never knew you hankered to be a cattle raiser. You should've took it up before you went after my brother. Then you could have kept on growing your cows."

"Your brother was a job I had to do," Dunn said coldly. "Same as all the others."

"One time you picked the wrong job," Greavey said. "Anyway, it don't change nothing. He's still dead and you're the man that killed him. Leaves it all up to me."

"No point to it," Dunn said. "It's a long time gone. If I kill you here, today, or you kill me, what's gained?"

Greavey's pale eyes narrowed. "What gives you the idea that you'll be getting any chance at me?"

Dunn shrugged. "I know you, Jay. And all your kind. I'll have my chance to draw. One thing you've got to find out is whether you're faster than me. If you just shot me down, you'd always wonder about it. And wondering about something like that eats away at a man like you."

"You're mighty cocksure," Greavey said. "Been a few years since you done your bounty hunting."

"But I kept my hand in. I've been expecting you. Knew you'd show, sooner or later."

"No! No!" Laura cried suddenly and flung

herself on Dunn.

He caught her in his arms, gently pushed her aside for the second time. At her unexpected movement, Greavey's sorrel shied violently, almost fell.

Dunn faced the gunman. "There's no call for this," he said when the horse had quieted down. "But if you will have it, let's get on with it."

Greavey said, "Fine. Just you stand quiet. Soon as I get on the ground, I'll holster my iron and we'll start from scratch."

Dunn only nodded. He wished there was some way he could persuade Laura to leave, but knew it was useless to try. He watched Greavey, gun still in hand and leveled at him, shift his weight to his left, and prepare to dismount. At that change, the skittish animal danced off to the right and began to back.

"Whoa!" Greavey yelled. "Whoa, damn you!"

The sorrel suddenly was on the rim of the arroyo. His right rear hoof missed the edge, pawed frantically in the air. Abruptly he was off balance, began scrambling for footing.

Greavey shouted another curse at the thoroughly-frightened animal. He brought his weapon about in a swift arc, endeavored to line it up on Dunn. Loose rock and earth broke out from under the frantic horse. He started to fall, threshing wildly. Greavey fired, determined to settle with Dunn in any event. The bullet went high, passed well above Ben's head, as the gunman and the sorrel tipped over backwards into the ravine.

13

Ben Dunn reacted quickly.

He drew his pistol, stepped to the edge of the arroyo. The sorrel was struggling to his feet. The whites of his eyes mirrored his fright and his jaws slavered froth. Beyond him lay Jay Greavey. He was spread-eagled on the ground, his gun half-buried in the sand where it had fallen. His head had struck a stone. Either he was dead or unconscious.

Dunn looked down upon the man who was determined to kill him. It could end there. With a single bullet he could close a door to the past, eliminate forever, perhaps, the possibility of trouble arising to haunt him again. He studied the senseless Greavey for a long minute. And then with a shrug he slid his revolver into his holster and wheeled about.

Laura had been watching him. He saw relief spread over her features, knew she had read the thoughts that had passed through his mind. She was glad of his decision. She ran to him, threw her arms about him, and for a time they were locked in an embrace. Finally he took her shoulders between his broad hands, held her at arm's length.

"We can't stay here. It's not safe. Marr and his bunch are somewhere close. And he," he added, nodding at Greavey, "won't sleep long."

"Where can we go?"

"Farther up the mountain. We can watch better from there. Soon as it's safe, we'll move on. It's going to be a race from here on."

"To Salt River?"

He said, "That's it. We've got enough proof now, I think, to back our story. Anyway, we'll try it on the marshal. If he won't listen, we'll telegraph the United States Marshal in El Paso. I know him."

They turned, took up the reins of their horses and, on foot, started along the edge of the ravine. They came to a break in its wall, dropped down into the sandy depth, crossed over and gained the opposite side. There they swung to the saddle and, favoring their mounts, began to ascend the long slope.

The day was growing on to noon. Heat

and thirst were beginning to make themselves felt. There was a canteen on Pete Frisco's saddle but it was empty. It would remain so; for they were heading away from the spring, and there was not another on that side of Comanche Mountain.

Behind him, Dunn heard Laura ask, "What will that Greavey do when he comes to? Will he —"

"Look for me?" Ben supplied the words. "Sure. He'll just start over again. Might join up with Marr or he could try to pick up our trail on his own."

"Oh." The word was a complete expression of her disappointment. "I thought that maybe, when he sees that you didn't go ahead and kill him, while he was lying there, he would be grateful enough to ride on and forget about you."

Ben shook his head. "Not Greavey, nor any of his kind. Sure, he'll be grateful, but not that much. He'll figure he owes me a favor, but it won't change what he thinks he has to do."

A sob wrenched from her lips. "I almost wish you had gone ahead and killed him when you had the chance. All this terrible hunting and shooting and killing — it's not human!"

He dropped back to her side. "Maybe," he

said. "But I couldn't have done it. It would have been cold-blooded murder. No matter who Greavey is or what he figures to do to me, I couldn't do it. And you wouldn't have wanted me to."

"I know," she murmured. "I just forgot myself for a moment. Oh, Ben, I'm about at my wits end! I don't think I can stand much more of this."

"You won't need to," he replied. "This time tomorrow, you'll be safe in Salt River."

The slope had begun to steepen, the horses to labor. Dunn halted, came down from the saddle. He helped Laura do the same.

"Better give the horses a breather. I should have borrowed that sorrel of Greavey's and left him this horse of Pete Frisco's. He's about done for."

Laura said nothing. She sank down in the narrow shade of a lightning-blasted stump. "Can we rest here for a little?"

"Better place higher up," he said. "A ledge where we can watch below for quite a ways. We've got to be on the lookout for Marr and the others. It's only a short walk."

She said, "I'm so tired. Seems like weeks since I had any sleep."

"Once we're on the ledge, you can have your sleep," he promised.

They resumed the climb, still leading the bay and Frisco's spent buckskin. Soon they broke out into a small clearing beneath the hogback. It was too steep at that point to scale, and they cut left, following along the base of the rock ledge until it faded into the body of the mountain itself. From there it was fairly simple to quarter the slope and drop back upon the shelf.

Ben led the way to its widest point, to where it jutted out at its farthest, and there stopped. He picketed the horses back in the trees, where there was grazing to be had, and returned to Laura. He raked up a quantity of dead leaves and pine needles, shaped up a bed for her in the shade of a towering spruce. She thanked him, crawled onto it at once. He kissed her lightly and moved to the edge of the ridge to take up his post. She was asleep before he had settled himself.

Midday wore by. The after hours, hot and hushed, began. From time to time, he dozed, catlike, taking his rest as he could but never for more than a few minutes at one length. He kept a sharp surveillance on the slope and the level ground far below, watching for Jay Greavey, or Marr's party sweeping back in an all out search.

He could think of nothing better than going on to Salt River and endeavoring to enlist the aid of the law, in one form or another. He could see no point in doubling back to the Loveless place. He had involved them too deeply now, and to call on them again for any help would only bring them more trouble. He hoped Sabine and his two companions had not done the couple any bodily harm; he could help them rebuild their house and sheds, but there was nothing he could do toward shouldering any suffering — except take revenge.

Getting to Salt River would be no easy chore. They first must have a canteen of water, and then some food. And a horse for Laura. His own bay likely could make the trip if not pressed too hard, but the buckskin that had been Pete Frisco's was out of the question. He cursed himself silently again for not swapping mounts with Jay Greavey when he had had the opportunity.

There was one answer: swing over to his own place. There he could obtain food and water and a fresh horse for the girl. He could even exchange the one he rode.

The problem and course of action settled in his mind, he lay back, continued to rest and maintain his vigil. When the sun reached its mid-afternoon position, he arose, went to where Laura slept. He shook her gently.

She sat up instantly, alarmed. "Is there trouble?"

He said, "No. Just time to leave."

He moved on by her to where the horses waited. He took up the reins, led them to the ledge. "We'll go to my ranch first," he said, helping her mount. While she settled herself, he explained the plan.

She felt much better for her rest and showed it. "Are we far from there?"

"Couple of hours," he replied and swung onto his bay. "Not a lot of miles but rough going. We have to take it slow."

They kept fairly high on the side of Comanche Mountain. There was no trail, only the unmarked slope. There were times when they were forced to drop lower or climb higher to circumvent an impassable outcropping of rock or some deep, storm-gouged canyon.

Eventually they were in more familiar surroundings, and Ben Dunn sought out the less arduous routes but never forsook an alert vigilance for comfort. They reached the southernmost boundary of his property and there started a gradual descent, working their way downward to level ground.

Abruptly, Dunn pulled to a halt.

"What is it?" Laura asked, moving quickly

to his side. "Did you hear something?"

He shook his head. "No, I thought I smelled smoke."

A frown creased his face. His jaw settled into a hard angle. "Come on. We're close so we'll have to go quiet. Might be someone around."

He feared that less than he did the persistent suspicion that now crowded his mind. Minutes later, when they halted at the edge of the clearing in which his ranch buildings sat, he saw that what he had feared, had come true.

His house, his small barn, all that he owned were little more than charred, smoking embers. The Box B had been burned to the ground.

And there were no horses.

14

For a long time he sat in absolute silence staring at the ruins. All he had worked for was gone. All he owned, except for the clothing on his back, the stock and the land itself, had been ruthlessly taken from him.

"Three years," he murmured, "down a hole."

He felt Laura touch his arm, heard her say, "Ben, I'm sorry. I feel it's my fault. If I hadn't dragged you into this, it never would have happened."

His dark face was set. "Maybe — and maybe not. I know Jack Marr's kind. This whole country wouldn't be big enough for him, once he got the fever to grab, and grow. Someday he would have found another excuse."

"It must have been Sabine and those other two men. Probably did this when they came back from the Loveless place. Fire has been out for some time."

He agreed. But he was not thinking so much of his loss, now the initial shock was over, as he was of their immediate circumstance. Without at least one fresh horse, the journey to Salt River was out of the question. And they could not remain there; Marr and his crew would be searching for them on one hand, the flat-eyed gunman, Jay Greavey, on the other.

"Wait here," he said. "I'll have a look around."

He pulled the bay about, faded off into the brush. There was a chance, a slim one, that his horses were close by. He recalled that Sabine and his two friends had ridden into Diamond X with no extra mounts, that Pete Frisco had been astride a horse he had taken from Abner Loveless. It was possible, he reasoned, that they had simply hazed the animals out of the barn and driven them off into the forest.

After several minutes search, he failed to turn up any of them. Disappointed, he circled back to Laura, after assuring himself there was no one else lurking nearby. Rejoining her, he again looked over his desolated holdings. The well had been spared, he noted. Even men such as Bibo Sabine hesitated to destroy, in any way, that priceless necessity in the west — water.

"Guess we can still get a drink," he said and led the way around the charred remains to the small housing that sheltered the well. They dismounted and secured the horses. He dropped the bucket down the narrow shaft, reeled it up. He served Laura. When she finished, he satisfied his own thirst and then provided for the two horses. While they drank greedily, he walked out into the center of the blackened ruins.

Squares of stone marked the foundations upon which his three rooms had rested. In the ashes he saw the remnants of a few possessions: the misshapen, blackened pot and pans; the kitchen stove. There lay the barrel of his shotgun with the wooden stock burned away, the skeleton of his other pistol.

He kicked it with the toe of his boot, reached down and picked it up. Here was the gun that had driven him there, he thought bitterly. Now it would be one like it, the so carefully matched mate, that would take him away — perhaps forever. He had no illusions as to what lay ahead. If it were only Jay Greavey that was to be faced, it would be a different matter. But Jack Marr, with a half a dozen gunslingers at his side, was something else.

His one hope was that Jay Greavey would stay clear of it, would not show up to prevent his squaring accounts with the Diamond X crew. He needed to do that, not only for himself but for Laura, as well. If there was nothing to be salvaged of his own life, he could at least help her. That was just what he would be doing if he erased Marr from the picture.

He should be taking steps to insure that. Marr would be back, he was certain. They would come looking for him there, sooner or later. This time they would find him, ready and waiting.

He wheeled, walked back slowly to the well where Laura waited in silence. He unhooked the canteen from Frisco's saddle, filled it. Tightening the cap, he hung it on the bay.

He squatted down before Laura, picked up a twig. "Look, I'll show you how to reach Salt River."

She dropped to his side. "Salt River?" she echoed, her voice rising with surprise. "I thought we were going together!"

"There's only one horse that can make it. You take him. I'll hang around here until I can get my hands on another. Then I'll follow."

She frankly distrusted his words. "Another? Where will you get another horse?"

He shrugged. "Figure there's a chance one

of mine will come wandering back. Horses sometimes do that along about dark."

"Then why can't I just wait?"

"I said it was just a chance. Could be tomorrow or the next day before I'll find one. Best you get started right away."

He drew a square in the moist earth. "Here's where we are now. And here's the mountain. You head out south on the trail and follow it until you are on the other side of the mountain. The trail forks there. Take the right hand and it will lead you to Salt River. Understand?"

She said, "Yes, but I don't want to go and leave you."

"Only thing to do," he said. "Anyway, quick as I get a horse, I'll follow. Likely to catch up to you before you've gone halfway."

He reached into his pocket, drew forth several coins. He handed them to her. "This will get you a room at the hotel and buy you meals at the restaurant." He paused, scratched in the soft earth with the stick. "Come to think of it, when you get there go first to that lawyer who's got an office next to the bank. Can't recall his name but he knows me. I had him draw up some papers for me once.

"You tell him what's happened and that I sent you to him. Show him that Bible and

146

the things we found in it. Tell him what you're up against."

"And I shouldn't go to the marshal?"

"Let him decide that. I figure you're better off to talk to him first, just in case Marr has already sent word to the marshal. He'll know what's best to do."

"You'll come as soon as you can?"

"Soon as I can," he said. "Don't push the bay too hard and he'll make it. You won't have to run him. I'll see that nobody follows you."

She looked at him more closely. A frown darkened her features. "You are expecting more trouble, aren't you? And one reason you're staying behind is so I can go free."

"We've got just one horse," he reminded her. "If we had another that could make it, I'd be right with you."

"I still think I should wait for you —"

He rose to his feet. "Do as I say," he said in a firm but gentle voice. "I know what I'm doing. You had better get started. Be dark in a couple of hours."

He turned to where the bay waited, pulled loose the reins. "Remember, don't crowd your horse and he'll be all right. Sure you got the directions right?"

"I'm sure," she murmured and moved up to him. She reached out, pulled his head down to a level with hers, kissed him full on the lips. "Don't be too long in coming. I won't rest easy until I see you again."

He grinned. "You just get to Salt River and that lawyer. That's all you need worry about."

"I don't want the ranch," she said, "not unless I can be with you. I'd rather give it up . . ."

Her words trailed off, faded from his consciousness. Movement in the brush beyond the clearing halted his awareness of all else. His eyes swung about in a brief circle. There were riders — Diamond X riders — all around them, encircling them. It was suddenly too late for all things.

15

Jack Marr, Pete Frisco, Bibo Sabine — a dozen others. They were there, every last one of them. They had eased about, now enclosed them in a silent, almost complete circle. Marr rode forward a dozen paces. Frisco and Sabine flanked him. Marr glanced casually at the blackened remains of the Box B.

"Boys did a right good job here, don't you think so, Dunn?"

Ben made no reply. A wild hate was tearing at his insides, flaring through his eyes. He moved a slow step away from Laura. Jack Marr was a dead man, whether he knew it or not. Sabine and Frisco would get in their shots, but not before he blasted the sneering Marr from his saddle.

"Knew you'd show up here again," Marr said. "Told the boys so. You're not very smart, mister."

Dunn remained silent, still not trusting

himself much. In the hush that followed Marr's words, one of the horses shifted his weight, blew noisily. Leather creaked in its dry way. Tension suddenly was a tangible element, evident as the sky itself. Through it Ben Dunn was desperately seeking to come up with an answer to a new problem that now faced him — how to get Laura safely free and away from the inevitable showdown that was coming?

"Tell me something, Dunn," Marr said, slouching to one side of his saddle, "did you actually think you and your woman could get away with it?"

"We weren't trying to get away with anything!" Laura exclaimed, finding her voice. "You know that! And we aren't guilty of doing anything wrong!"

Marr laughed. That sound was immediately taken up and echoed by Sabine and Frisco.

"I'll say this," Marr observed in mock admiration, "you're a hard one to put off, lady. And a cool one. You'd have to be to stick a knife in an old, sick man."

"That's a lie," Dunn snapped. "She didn't do it, and you know it. I reckon you know who did."

"Maybe it was you then, if it wasn't her."

"He wasn't even on the ranch, not after

he left that morning," Laura said. "You can't blame Ben for any of this. I got him into it, and he was only trying to help me. You must believe that!"

"I believe what I know," Marr began.

"But you're wrong about Ben!" Laura cried, her voice rising. "Do what you want with me! Keep the ranch, have me arrested for murder — but leave Ben out of it!"

"Don't waste your breath," Dunn said. "Marr knows what the truth is and that he's got to bury it with us — both of us. I won't have you beg him for my life."

"That there truth you're talkin' about," an older rider, apparently one of Isaac Pope's original hired hands, was speaking, "what you figure it is?"

Dunn saw Marr throw an angry glance at the cowboy. Before that man could speak, he said, "The truth is this: we didn't have anything to do with Pope's murder. And this is his daughter, Laura."

Marr quickly resumed control of the moments. He shrugged. "What else you expect him to say? Sure, he'll deny any charges we make. Wouldn't you if you were about to be strung up?"

Complete silence followed that. Marr waited a time, half turned in his saddle. "Harvey, you got those ropes?"

The tall rider came in nearer. He took the two lariats coiled loosely over his saddle horn, handed one to Sabine, the other to Frisco.

At sight of that, Laura uttered a small cry, turned to Ben and threw her arms about him. He held her for a moment, then moved her aside. When she was out of the way, he faced Marr. His hand hung close to the pistol at his hip.

Marr read his mind. "Don't try it," he warned softly. "There's half a dozen guns on you. And they won't shoot to kill, only to stop you from doing anything foolish. We're going to hang you, Dunn. You and your lady friend, too. That's the kind of justice you deserve and are going to get."

"Now, wait a minute here," the older puncher who had spoken up before, broke in. "I don't know about this hangin' a woman —"

"What's the difference, Earl?" Marr demanded impatiently. "They were both in on it. They tried to euchre Pope out of his ranch by her claiming to be his daughter. When that didn't work, one of them killed him. And then to make it worse, they broke in and robbed the house while we were off burying the old man. If all that doesn't call for a hanging, I'd sure like to know what does!"

"He's a liar," Dunn stated calmly. "We had nothing to do with the murder. We were in the house during the funeral. We don't deny it. But we weren't robbing it. We were trying to find the proof we need to show that Laura is the daughter of Isaac Pope."

"Which you didn't find," Marr said.

Dunn nodded. "We didn't find it because you had already taken it."

Marr stirred. "No, because there wasn't any in the first place. That's just talk."

"Not quite," Dunn said coolly. "We found something that —"

"You boys throw those ropes over that limb there," Marr broke in hastily. "Might as well hang them from the same tree. They run together, we'll let them swing together."

"Now, hold on, Jack!" Earl yelled and rode forward from his position in the brush. "I'm for makin' anybody pay that killed Isaac, but I ain't so danged sure about this. And I ain't sure about hangin' a woman! I figure we better let the law have a hand in this."

Marr's voice was abruptly harsh. "Keep out of this, old man. If you're too chicken-hearted to do what's got to be done, then ride out. Go on back to the ranch and milk your cows."

Earl plucked at his stringy mustache. "Appears to me you're in an all-fired hurry to do this, Jack. You got some reason?"

"Reason? Here are two people who killed my Pa in cold blood, and you ask me for a reason!"

The old cowboy moved his bony shoulders and spat. "Well, I don't reckon there's a argument against that, but I still don't cotton to stringin' up a woman. And they's some more of the boys here I 'spect feel the same way."

Harvey and another rider moved in behind Jack Marr. With Sabine and Frisco, they instantly became a tight, small group, threatening and ready for anything.

Marr said, "Earl, maybe you and the men you mentioned are tired of working for the Diamond X — and me. Maybe this would be a good time for you to pull stakes."

"Could be," the old puncher replied agreeably. He studied the five men for a time. "You know, things ain't been right around the ranch since old Isaac got sick and you took over, Jack. It sure ain't no fittin' place for a man to work cows no more. I'll just take your advice and give my notice now —"

"I don't need any notice," Marr snapped. "Just be gone by the time I get back. If you got any wages coming, tell Harrison I said to pay you off." He pivoted about, threw his attention along the circle of riders. "Goes for all the rest of you, too. Now's the time to leave, if you've a mind to!"

Dunn, silent through the exchange and encouraged by the stubborn opposition on the part of Earl, saw another hope begin to dwindle away. He cast about for some means to hold the dissenters. He came up with a question.

"Any of you remember Pope had a wife?"

Earl, in the act of pulling away from the clearing, halted. He frowned, stared at Dunn. "Reckon I'm the oldest about the place and I don't recollect no such thing. Course, I come to work for Isaac about three years after he started up. Could have been before."

"Forget it," Marr cut in. "Move on, old man. I'm tired of your yammering. Pete, you and Bibo throw those ropes over that limb. Let's get on with this."

Dunn's attention swung to Marr. His face was stiff, grimly set. These were the last moments Laura and he would know. Of that he was certain. But he would make them count.

"They do," he said to Marr, "and you'll never live to see them finish the job. I promise you that, Marr."

"So? With a half a dozen slugs in you — what do you figure to do?"

"Still put one bullet in your heart," Dunn stated. "I'll have that much time."

From the edge of the clearing, Jay Greavey's voice said, "Hate to bust in on your little party, gents, but I claim first bite of this Dunn."

16

Startled, Marr swung about sharply. Sabine and Frisco again hesitated. Harvey, waiting for no cue, clawed at the pistol on his hip. A gunshot smashed through the hush. Harvey rocked on his saddle, sagged forward clutching at his shoulder.

Through a wisp of acrid powder smoke that drifted out into the clearing, Greavey said, "Seems there's always one joker that's got to prove how brave he is. Now, all of you just ease over there behind your boss, so's I can keep an eye on you better."

The riders who had formed the tight semicircle around Laura Pope and Dunn, immediately complied. They guided their mounts to positions back of and to the sides of Marr and the others.

"Fine, that's fine," Greavey drawled from his place beyond the screen of brush. "Don't know what this is all about but I reckon it's got something to do with the killing of that rancher."

Marr said, "You're right. They murdered Isaac Pope — my pa. We were about to string them up for it."

"The girl, too?" Greavey asked, faint surprise in his voice. "Well, no truck of mine. But Dunn, there, is. He's a big man when it comes to killing and if you figure he killed this Pope, then I reckon he sure did. But I come first. He shot down my brother and I've been a long time running him down to square that."

A glimmer of fresh hope rose within Ben Dunn; hope for Laura Pope, at least. He raised his arms, held his hands well away from his sides to indicate he had no intention of going for his gun. Deliberately, he pivoted about slowly, placed his back to Marr. He faced the point where Greavey, yet concealed, was standing.

"All right, Jay, you've caught up. I'm ready to have it out with you anytime you say. First, I'd like to make a bargain."

"A bargain?" Greavey said and laughed. "You ain't in such a good shape to bargain with me, Dunn."

"Not for myself, for the lady here. This whole thing is a trumped-up job. Marr there's no real kin of Isaac Pope, but the girl here actually is his daughter. And neither one of us killed him."

"Wondered about you using a knife," Greavey commented. "Never knew you worked that way."

"Laura is the rightful owner of that ranch but Marr here, and some of his private bunch are out to keep her from getting it."

"Some of them?"

"Yeh, the ones there in the middle. Rest of them ain't so sure. I'd like a chance to prove to them the girl is in the right."

Greavey did not immediately answer. Finally, "You trying to work some kind of a trick, Dunn?"

Ben shook his head. "No trick. Just don't want to see the girl get hurt. Once I've had my say, then it's you and me."

"Don't believe it!" Marr shouted. "He's got something up his sleeve!"

"How could I get away with anything?" Dunn demanded. "You're on one side of me, they're on the other. And all I'm asking for is a chance to talk a few minutes and show a couple of tintypes in a book to prove what I say is the truth."

Greavey again considered at length. "What's in it for you?"

"Nothing for me," Ben said. "All for the lady. Don't like to stand by and see her get the worst of a deal, if I can help it."

"All right," Greavey said. "Reckon I owe you a favor. You could have put a bullet in me back there in the hills when that damned horse of mine fell. But, I'm giving you warning; I don't trust you much. I'll be watching close; you make one wrong move, I'll break both your legs."

"You've got my word."

"Don't know if that's any good or not and it don't make any difference one way or another. I'll just do my depending on my irons." He paused, continued, "Now, the rest of you saddlewarmers, set quiet until he's done. You listen to what he's got to say. In case you can't see me plain, I'm standing here with a forty-five in each hand. I can empty both of them into the pack of you before you could pull back a hammer. Just remember that and do your listening."

Dunn felt Laura's eyes on him, searching, wondering. He grinned down at her, exhibiting a confidence he was not too certain of, himself.

"All right, bounty hunter," Greavey said, "it's your she-bang."

Dunn turned about, faced Marr and the silent group of Diamond X riders. "I don't figure to be much of a lawyer," he began, "and I've never had much practice talking out like this. But I reckon the truth is always

160

easy to speak out. You heard me say Laura Pope is the daughter of Isaac. And that we didn't have anything to do with killing him. Somebody else pulled that off to make it look bad for her. I don't think you'll have to go far to find out who's behind it. Figure a minute. If she is the heir of Pope, who would the Diamond X go to? Who would lose out?"

Dunn stopped, permitted the questions to have their effect. There was a stir among the riders.

"Reckon that would be Jack Marr," Earl said. "He'd lose out sure."

Ben nodded. "And right there's where I think you'll find the man who murdered Isaac Pope, or ordered it done."

There was a long minute of silence then Jack Marr found his voice. "That's a damn lie! He's trying to cover up. Pope never was married —"

"I've got proof that he was," Dunn said calmly. "And he had a daughter." He turned, looked toward the invisible Greavey. "I'll have to get that book strapped to my saddle."

The gunman said, "Get it for him, lady."

Laura stepped quickly to the bay horse, untied the leather strings. She returned with the thick Bible, handed it to Dunn.

Ben wheeled back to Marr and the others. He noted Sabine and Frisco no longer held ropes. The coils now hung loosely over their saddles, leaving their hands free. He wondered if Greavey had also noticed the change.

He opened the book to its front page, held it up. "Here's the Pope family record. Shows the date he was married and gives the name of his wife. Then it shows a daughter was born. One of you step up here and take a look."

There was no response to the request. Finally Earl said, "Go on, Tom. Reckon you read letterin' better'n the rest of us. See what it says."

A young cowboy stirred himself, dismounted. He shouldered by Marr, halted a few steps from Dunn, glanced questioningly in Greavey's direction.

"Go right ahead," the gunman said. "Just keep your hands where I can see them."

The rider moved up to Ben who still held the book extended for him to see. He examined it for a few moments, stepped back.

"Sure what it says," he announced, facing Earl and the rest. "Dates and all are there."

"Means nothing," Marr said. "Anybody could have written that in. The girl herself could have done it after they took that book from the house."

"How about these pictures then?" Dunn said and leafed to the back of the Bible where the tintype likenesses were framed in their ovals and squares. "You figure we did them, too?"

Tom studied the pages carefully. He scratched at his head, faced his friends. "He's sure right. These here pictures show old Isaac with a wife and kid, a baby girl. And there's writing saying who they are."

"But nothing to prove this girl is the same as the one in the pictures," Marr added, a note of triumph in his voice. "Seems to me all we know now is that Pope was married and had a daughter. No more than that."

"When Laura got here, she had that proof," Dunn said. "She showed it to Pope and he accepted it, agreed that she was his daughter. There was a letter or two and a picture — one like these. But the night Pope was killed, it all disappeared. The picture, the letters, even the carpetbag she carried them in —"

"Carpetbag?" Earl exclaimed. "That wouldn't be the one I saw you burnin' in the fireplace, would it, Bibo?"

There was a moment of stunned silence as the full meaning of the old cowboy's question drove home in the minds of the others.

"By God, Dunn's right!" somebody finally said. "This girl is old Isaac's daughter. And she wouldn't have done no killin'."

Ben felt a brief glow of satisfaction, of relief. Then he saw Sabine and Frisco suddenly hunch forward. He brushed Laura to one side with a sweep of his arm. His gun came up fast, bucked in his hand. He saw Marr level down on him even as he threw his first bullets into Sabine and Frisco.

Behind him he was vaguely aware of other guns firing, realized that Jay Greavey was having his say. He set himself for the smash of lead into his back. Miraculously, there was none. Marr was falling from the saddle. Sabine was down. Frisco had buckled forward, arms dangling on either side of his horse's neck. Harvey had made no move to become a part of the skirmish. Like all the others, he sat with hands lifted. Understanding came then to Ben Dunn. Greavey had not fired on him, but had backed his play.

He drew himself up slowly. Keeping clearly in view of Greavey, he slid his revolver back into its holster. Laura, white and shaken, scrambled to her feet, rushed to him.

"Are you hurt?"

He said, "No, I'm fine." He swung his eyes to Marr, sprawled full length on the ground. "But I reckon that's all for Jack. And for Bibo and Pete."

"Oh, I'm so thankful!" she cried, throwing her arms about him. "All those guns! It was terrible — horrible!"

"It's over with now," he said, comforting her. He turned his attention to Earl and the remaining Diamond X men. "I take it you're satisfied the lady is Laura Pope?"

The old puncher bobbed his head. "Ain't no doubt! Everything sure fits. And I allow it was Bibo that done the killin'. He looked after them kind of chores for Jack."

"Then take her home," Dunn said. "And have your boys load up those bodies and give them a burying."

He felt her stiffen against him. "I won't go," she delcared and clung to him. "I won't leave — I love you, Ben."

He held her close for a long minute. In that brief time the grim lines of his face softened and, as quickly, hardened.

"Take her," he said brusquely to Earl, who stood nearby. "And don't let her come back here."

He pulled away from the girl, wheeled toward the waiting Jay Greavey. He heard her sob and plead with the old cowpuncher to let her go.

"I can't — I won't!" she cried.

He deafened himself to the sound of her voice and walked on.

17

He halted near the center of the clearing. He did not move, nor did the gunman, until Laura and the others had ridden away. Only then did Jay Greavey show himself. He emerged from the brush, holstered his left-side gun. The right was yet in his hand. He pulled to a stop a few paces in front of Dunn.

"You're a regular holy joe!" he said, a sneer on his lips. "A real, genuine do-gooder. You changed some since the old days."

"Everything changes," Dunn said. "A thing you ought to realize."

"Tom's still dead," Greavey replied coldly. "Ain't nothing going to change that."

"And you think a shoot-out with me will?"

"Maybe not — except you'll be dead, same as him."

The small talk had begun to grind on Ben Dunn's nerves. He said, "Let's get on with it. No sense in standing here, doing all this jawing."

"You in a hurry to die?" the gunman asked. He was taking some sort of enjoyment from the delay. "You figure to go somewheres afterwards?"

"Maybe."

"Don't count on it," Greavey said. "I can take you, Dunn, any day in the week. If I didn't figure it so, I'd put a bullet in you now. But I want you to do some thinking these last few minutes while you're alive. Some thinking about that kid brother of mine."

"He was as bad as the worst of them. You know that."

"Got nothing to do with it. You started something you couldn't finish, and it's got to be settled by me."

Dunn shrugged. "You got that stuck in your mind. Like all your kind. Man sets himself up to believe a thing is one way. Was like that with me until a few days ago. Kept thinking about what had happened, what had gone before. Then it all changed.

"I found out it was easy to think about the present, even make a few plans for the future. Sure, I know a man can't get away from the past, but he don't have to keep on living it. And that's what you're doing.

168

You're still living and fighting what used to be."

Greavey cocked his head in mock admiration. "You ought to have been one of them lawyers, instead of a bounty hunter!"

"You'd know what I say is true, if you'd let yourself think it over. What's done is done and us standing-to in a gun-fight won't prove anything now. Never has and never will. About all a man can do about the past is regret it — but there it ends."

Jay Greavey fondled the well-worn weapon in his hands. He hooked his right forefinger in the trigger guard, spun it expertly, "You wouldn't be trying to talk me out of killing you, would you, bounty man?"

Dunn said, "No. With a single track mind like you've got, you'd just go off somewhere, think about it for a spell, then come back. Your kind never learns anything until it's too late."

"Only time it's too late for a man is when he's dead."

"That's what I mean."

"You through talking out?"

"I'm ready when you are," Dunn replied.

"Gun of yours is about empty. You want to reload?"

"One bullet left in it. All I need."

Dunn saw the briefest flicker of uncertainty pass through Greavey's eyes and vanish. The gunman forced a laugh. "Mighty sure of yourself. You figure to get me with one bullet, that it?"

"Only takes one to kill a man."

Again Ben Dunn saw that moment of doubt in the gunman's gaze. He smiled faintly. "Thought you were in a hurry?"

Greavey shook his head. "Was just thinking about that woman. Sure going to be a shame, making her a widow before she even has a chance to marry up."

"Way the cards fall. She's a fine girl."

"Once knew a good woman —" Greavey began but Dunn's voice sliced through his words.

"Anytime, Jay."

The gunman's lips settled into a thin line. He began to back away, slowly, taking careful, precise half steps. Dunn remained motionless. He felt the man's eyes lock to his own, hold.

He saw a motion off to his right, beyond Jay Greavey. Abner Loveless walked into the clearing. He held an old, single barrel shotgun in his hands. It was pointed at Greavey.

"Hold up there, mister!" the old puncher rasped. "What's this here all about, Ben?"

The gunman came to a halt. He did not

remove his steady gaze from Dunn, merely suspended all movement.

"Raise up your hands!" Loveless ordered, walking in a step nearer.

It was a way out, an easy way. That thought flashed through Ben Dunn's mind as he saw Greavey slowly lift his arms. He didn't know if he could match the gunman's speed with a revolver or not; there was a good chance he could fail, that he would die in the shoot-out. A man can get rusty, go stale. But to call it off solved nothing. It was not the answer, for Greavey would come again; he would have his try.

He said, "Forget it, Abner. Stay out of this."

The shotgun in Loveless' hands lowered. "That what you want?"

"It's what I want."

Dunn watched Greavey. The gunman's arms dropped slowly to his sides. His face was expressionless, only that dead, empty stare. He had found a distance and position to his liking and no longer backed away. Ben shut out all else from his consciousness, concentrated on Greavey alone. He tried to recall what he knew of the man, of his style. Was he the sort who lunged to one side when he fired? Or did he dip forward, go down low as so many fast guns were inclined to do? He could not remember. It had been so long ago.

Suddenly Greavey was in action. His right hand was an upsweeping blur. His body twisted slightly left. Dunn threw himself forward. His own weapon smashed out its sound, even before he completed the move.

He felt Greavey's bullet drive into his shoulder and weathered the spasm of pain as it shattered bone. He saw Greavey spin on, complete a full turn. He realized his slug had caught the gunman as he twisted. Greavey went to his knees, struggled to rise. His mouth was open, his features distorted. He fought to lift the gun in his hand and level it. Abruptly he was without strength. He fell heavily, going full length.

Numbed by the bullet, Dunn stood motionless while Abner Loveless crossed the clearing, halted beside the gunman. He kicked Greavey's revolver off into the brush, peered down into the man's chalk-white face.

"He's dead," the old puncher said, straightening up. "You got him almost dead center. What was this here ruckus all about? Don't recollect ever seein' him around before."

"An old score," Ben said, "finally settled." His head was beginning to spin a little. He walked slowly to the well, leaned against the wooden housing.

"You and Hopeful all right?" he asked. "Heard you'd been burned out."

"We're all right," Loveless said. "Say, looks like you're hit right good." He swung around, faced the brush. "Hopeful, come over h'yar! Ben's gone and got hisself shot. Needs some doctorin'."

Abner poured a dipper of water, held it to Dunn's lips. "You need somethin' stronger'n this, but I reckon it'll have to do."

Hopeful Loveless came bustling into the clearing. She had apparently been waiting in the brush until Abner was sure of what was taking place. She began at once to tend his wound, making little clucking noises as she worked.

Abner glanced about the yard. "I'd say old Bibo and Pete and that other feller paid you a little visit, too," he remarked. "Say, where's the little gal?"

"Riding for the Pope place," Dunn said. He related the previous encounter which had ended up with the death of Marr and his two men. "Everything is squared around for her now. Guess Diamond X has got a new boss."

Abner Loveless was looking beyond him, to the edge of the clearing. "Maybe so, but

173

she sure ain't headed for her ranch."

Dunn was suddenly aware of Laura's presence at his side. He turned to face her.

"I had to come," she said. "When I heard those gunshots, I had to come back. Oh, Ben, are you hurt bad?"

"Bullet in the shoulder, that's all."

"Be all right, soon as we get him to some doctoring," Hopeful said, completing the bandage.

"Then it's all over and done with," Laura said in a thankful voice.

Dunn glanced at Greavey. "He's only one. Likely there will be more."

"We won't worry about them," she said. "And if they come, we'll face them together. Right now we've got to get you to our ranch and take care of your arm."

"Where?" he wondered.

She smiled at him. "To our ranch," she repeated. "And we've got plenty of room for Abner and Hopeful if they want to come along."

The old cowboy grinned broadly. "I reckon you just hired yourself a couple of new hands, ma'am," he said. "Let's get started for home!"

ABOUT THE AUTHOR

Ray Hogan was born in the Jesse James country of Missouri, where his father was a lawman. With that kind of a start, it seemed pretty inevitable that he'd wind up writing Westerns, especially after his family moved to Albuquerque, New Mexico, where Ray grew up, married, and still resides. He started writing in 1950, sold extensively to the Western magazines, then turned to novel-writing. He has been quite successful at that, and Ace Books have published many of his fine books.

Ray has a son, a daughter, and two grandchildren. He holds down a full-time job as a salesman for a truck agency, writes in his spare time, and in his time off (when?) is an ardent hunter and fisherman, turns out a weekly rod-and-gun column for the *Albuquerque Tribune,* and is an official of the National Wildlife Federation.

We hope you have enjoyed this Large Print book. Other Thorndike, Wheeler, Kennebec, and Chivers Press Large Print books are available at your library or directly from the publishers.

For information about current and upcoming titles, please call or write, without obligation, to:

Publisher
Thorndike Press
295 Kennedy Memorial Drive
Waterville, ME 04901
Tel. (800) 223-1244

or visit our Web site at:

http://gale.cengage.com/thorndike

OR

Chivers Large Print
published by BBC Audiobooks Ltd
St James House, The Square
Lower Bristol Road
Bath BA2 3SB
England
Tel. +44(0) 800 136919
email: bbcaudiobooks@bbc.co.uk
www.bbcaudiobooks.co.uk

All our Large Print titles are designed for easy reading, and all our books are made to last.